An unexpected wedding—hers!

"Attention, everyone. The bride has arrived."

Greg's grandfather's voice boomed around the room as Jane stepped into the huge, opulent living room of green and gold, and froze. The room was alive with people! And decorated like a mini wedding chapel!

Bride? Yes, and witnesses.... Jane absorbed the scene and its meaning in slow motion. *Her own wedding was in progress.* Details like the guest list had been chosen for her. As had the gift preference, she realized, noting the silver-and-white packages on display atop the antique supper table.

Boy, oh boy, did she need a new can opener. But she was relatively certain that the treasures beneath the wrappings were pricey and useless. In all fairness, it would be tough to choose a gift for Greg, a man who owned his own department store.

She released a nervous giggle. She wasn't getting married to Greg, and she'd be buying her own damn can opener!

She couldn't have been more wrong....

Leandra Logan spent her high school years clerking in various department stores in the Twin Cities, and often wondered if there were any eligible bachelors on the executive floor. An employee discount, however, was the only perk she ever received, until her memories inspired this story.

Don't miss Leandra's third title in her baby theme trilogy, *Angel Baby,* available late in 1995.

Books by Leandra Logan

HARLEQUIN TEMPTATION
362—DILLON AFTER DARK
393—THE LAST HONEST MAN
433—THE MISSING HEIR
472—JOYRIDE
491—HER FAVORITE HUSBAND
519—HAPPY BIRTHDAY, BABY

HARLEQUIN AMERICAN ROMANCE
559—SECRET AGENT DAD

BARGAIN BASEMENT BABY
LEANDRA LOGAN

Best Wishes, Gay,

Leandra Logan

Harlequin Books

TORONTO • NEW YORK • LONDON
AMSTERDAM • PARIS • SYDNEY • HAMBURG
STOCKHOLM • ATHENS • TOKYO • MILAN
MADRID • WARSAW • BUDAPEST • AUCKLAND

For Cathy Kohman,
a longtime friend who
appreciates both sparkling wine and
sparkling conversation

ISBN 0-373-25635-3

BARGAIN BASEMENT BABY

Copyright © 1995 by Mary Schultz.

Prologue

May 1975

IT WAS A LOVELY DAY for a wedding.

Even with only four scant weeks for preparation, the Baron affair held an impressive air of propriety. This was due in great part to the hushed dignity of the grand old chapel, the presence of St. Paul's social leaders, and of course, the Barons themselves. The family represented old Minnesota money and the name commanded respect from all those who shopped in their downtown Emporium—St. Paul's oldest and largest department store.

The groom had the Barons' good standing in the community in mind when he bowed to his parents' wishes and put his nuptials in their hands. Twenty-year-old Gregory, heir to the family fortune, would have preferred a small campus wedding back at U.C.L.A., where he and his bride-to-be, Nicole Resnick, had just finished their junior year. Instead, he'd flown back home to St. Paul with much of the wedding party in tow.

Despite the rushed schedule and the concessions made for his folks, Gregory was impressed with and appreciative of the results. He beamed, standing by the chapel's cool stone altar with his best man and best friend, Kevin Cross, and Nicole's brother Mark.

The tuxedoed trio shared similar traits. All were in keeping with the day's fashion, with their collar-length hair, generous sideburns and white suits with flared legs and lapels.

The groom managed to stand out just the same with an innate savvy and some very striking external features. His golden hair was bleached brilliant by the California sun and his jawline was sculptured strength beneath his suntanned skin.

But the gleaming gray eyes made the man—characteristically silvered with an excitement and anticipation that gazed far beyond the moment, into a future of his own design.

Greg liked to seize the moment, the day, with energized spontaneity. And this union was a good example of that. The decision to seize the hand of Nicole Resnick was an instinctive, abrupt decision. They'd taken several classes together during the past semester and discovered that they shared an adventurous spirit.

He flashed a fond look at his parents, Clark and Amanda, seated in the front pew. His thin, regal-looking father held his chin high as he stared straight ahead, probably praying for a sign—perhaps a strike of lightning—to jolt his son back to his senses before it was too late. His mother was dabbing her eyes beneath the brim of her sheer pink hat, overcome with a mixture of joy and uncertainty. They had been strongly opposed to this sudden leap into matrimony, pointing out that the couple had another year of college ahead of them, and hardly knew each other well enough to make a lifetime commitment.

Gregory realized that there was a more specific agenda on their minds. They wanted him to step right into department-store management next year, after graduation. To take his rightful place in line behind Clark as successor to Baron's Emporium. They worried that Nicole, who shared his love for communications, would spirit him off to investigate world happenings.

The elder Barons were absolutely right. But Nicole was only an enhancement to his own plans. The dream to document world events in an informative and entertaining way had been with him since junior high, when he made a movie about "a day in the life" of a department-store owner, namely, his father.

It was the moviemaking and not the job that had mesmerized young Greg. And he hadn't outgrown the preference. He had no interest in settling down in his father's seventh-floor offices to help Sir—as most called him—dictate departmental policy to Emporium employees.

His grandfather had founded the store nearly sixty years ago. It had been his dream come true, then his father's dream come true. Greg, in turn, had endured a thorough apprenticeship from the Bargain Basement all the way upstairs.

It was all part of Sir's master plan. When he retired, he wanted Gregory there on standby, eager to take the helm of the store. But playing second fiddle to his robust forty-eight-year-old parent didn't interest Greg in the least. Clark Baron didn't need him right now any more than he needed a third hand between his shoulder blades. Amanda was there for him. She, too, spent her days at the Emporium, loving each and every minute of it.

They were the most wonderful parents a guy could ask for. If they'd just give him a chance to do things his own way...

Greg squared his shoulders as the organist in the choir loft plunged into a soulful rendition of a Carpenters tune.

Two bridesmaids in lavender started up the aisle. One was a friend of Nicole's, the other, Greg's cousin from Minneapolis.

She was right behind them.

A vision in white. A bouquet of yellow roses clasped in her hand, a woven coronet of the same flower set in her cloud of shiny dark curls.

He was riveted to her innocent beauty, overtaken by her hypnotizing wishpower.

Her hair was the bluest of black, her eyes the bluest of blue.

Her fragile little chin was set firmer than his father's.

She glided forward in time with the music. Sunshine splashed through high stained-glass windows, reflecting off her snowy tiered gown in a kaleidoscope of color.

The ladies in lavender made their approach, easing into place on the opposite side of the altar.

She, in turn, moved up into the front-and-center position, clenching her bouquet in a death grip.

Right on cue the song eddied away.

The chapel was held in a hushed moment, a ceremonial pause meant as a prelude to the big moment to follow.

Like a small keen animal, she was weighing her options. Her gaze was literally blazing blue fire beneath a thick sweep of raven lashes.

It was her last chance to take a chance.

He knew she was going to act, perhaps even before she did. Her fierce feelings for him had been played out so clearly during her march.

Her courage had surged stronger with every dainty footfall.

She now trembled with raw nerve.

He alone knew she was about to explode....

Her eyes never left his as she hoisted her ruffled hem to perilous heights and extended her lip to jutting extremes. He wanted to shout a word of caution, a small plea for restraint.

His jaw sagged slightly, but he felt helpless—as she always made him feel!

The seconds to follow were a mad scramble. The rustle of taffeta and clatter of patent-leather shoes echoed hollowly through the stone structure.

Tearing between the startled groomsmen, she made a daring leap for Gregory. He caught her in midair, holding her close as she wound her arms around his broad, suited shoulders. "You can't marry her! You're mine!"

The dashing groom of privilege gently cradled the little flower girl as she sobbed into his lapel. His sweet baby Jane. So much female at the tender age of five. Leave it to her to make this final-hour bid for him!

He reached up to stroke her soft black curls. "I'm an old man and you know it, pumpkin," he murmured in her ear.

"I'll get bigger," she promised on a sniffle. "You just gotta wait for me."

"I can't," he crooned. "I just can't."

"Sure you can!"

Gregory's gaze strayed back to the front pew reserved for family, where Jane's grandmother and guardian, Mabel Haley, was seated with his parents. The fiftyish blond Mabel, his mother's best friend and his father's private secretary, was working to conceal her amused expression behind a lacy kerchief. His folks, who held both Haleys in high esteem, were at a total loss, caught between sympathy and embarrassment.

Ironically, the child was reflecting their collective disapproval in the most basic form.

Just the same, it was no good for appearances.

Things like this just didn't happen to the Baron family. This event was slated to appear on the St. Paul *Clarion*'s society page, not the comics section!

Jane lifted her face to his, her chin quivering. "Grandma Mabbe don't mind. She said I could tell you."

He sighed in exasperation. "But I don't think she meant now, Janey."

"But I want you. I love you!"

Gregory held her close as she erupted in a fresh round of sobs. Janey was as spoiled as she was lovely, and accustomed to getting exactly what she wanted with charm and spunk. Her parents had been killed in a car accident three years ago and Mabel had taken her in—as had the Barons—encompassing her with all the love and security her little heart could hold. And all the self-confidence her little head could hold.

The child was brainwashed into believing everything was within her reach.

And she was reaching out for Gregory with all she had, fervently anticipating that, like everything else, he would be hers only for the asking.

But she was also devastated in a most heart-wrenching way.

She had a tremendous crush on him and it was all his fault. Like the other adults, he had teased her unmercifully and pampered her unreservedly.

A deeper cry suddenly tore through the church. It was the bride, standing in the back alcove on the arm of her father.

For a moment, Gregory had forgotten all about Nicole waiting in the wings for the organist's cue.

Nicole wasted no time storming up the aisle in a badly suppressed huff, her veil taking flight over her feathered blond hair. The organist swiftly dived into a choppy rendition of the "Wedding March."

It took four ushers and Grandma Mabel to pry Jane loose.

A sore loser or a determined winner? No matter how one put it, Janey had the final say. Even as they were hauling her through a side door, she was denouncing the union to the limits of her impressive five-year-old vocabulary.

Part wish. Part prediction.

Greg would wonder in the years to come if she had somehow put a spell on him with wishpower, binding him up in a loveless limbo, until she was good and ready to stake her claim all over again!

1

March 1995

ALL EYES WERE ON Jane Haley as she climbed the steep ladder of the red-and-blue plastic slide erected in the center of Baron's toy department. Whether it was because she was dressed in a clingy yellow leotard, or because she had just given the showiest sales pitch in the history of the Emporium was hard to say.

She hoped it was a combination of both.

Two decades had passed since her wild wedding-day bid for the only Baron heir, and she was at it again, garnering attention at the expense of the same family.

But it was strictly business, this time. After trying her hand at a variety of jobs—everything from gardener to telephone operator—Jane had decided to follow in her grandmother's footsteps. She'd joined the department-store team.

For the past three years, she'd apprenticed in all the different positions throughout the Emporium, first working in Sir's office at a clerical job, then in a number of departments, stocking, cleaning and selling. In the end she'd come to realize that sales was her niche. She loved people and she loved the challenge of influencing them. The thrill of the transaction, the satisfaction in commission. She had remarkable customer-service savvy, had her technique down to an art form. It was paying off, too. She'd finally worked her way through the ranks to a senior-clerk position in Toys, beneath only departmental manager, Desmond Nibling.

Business was all right, but she knew it could so easily be better. If the proper steps were taken to bring the department into the twentieth century!

Jane had felt she could do it single-handedly. Given free rein, she'd prove her theories.

This week had been her chance.

The haughty Mr. Nibling had done her the inadvertent favor of taking some sick leave. With some fevered sneezing and snorting, he'd announced at closing time on Tuesday that he would not be returning for the rest of the week.

In his absence she'd transformed the entire area into a circus of fun, a promotional extravaganza.

And spent two days planning for this event.

Every piece of Plas-Tek fine playground equipment sold in their catalog had been assembled. All five clerks had been assigned bright costumes. The athletic elfin Jane, with her lush mane of midnight-blue hair and trim compact body, had chosen her leotard and tutu with care. She wanted all eyes pinned on her alone as she personally demonstrated all the Plas-Tek features—the smooth safe corners, the easy cleanup, the vivid nonfading colors.

The ploy had been a rousing success. Up to this point.

She was just winding up her sales pitch from her perch at the top of the slide, when she suddenly spotted her superior, wending his way through the flock of curious customers.

The red-nosed and bleary-eyed Nibling, with Tuesday's rumpled black suit hanging on his narrow round-shouldered frame, his not-so-natty bow tie askew at his snowy collar, had undoubtedly been called out of his sickbed to pull in the reins on her. Some weak-kneed clerk in the department had finally mustered up the nerve to call in the boss.

But they had waited too long. Her goals were by and large accomplished. The customers already had Plas-Tek bro-

chures and helium balloons in hand. She'd touted everything there was to tout.

Nibling could put a stop to the show.

But he was too late to stop the sales.

Jane couldn't help cringing a bit under his stoked expression, however. A natural go-getter, she had only focused on
the positive results her stunt would bring. She gulped hard
as the possible consequences of her actions ran through her
mind for the first time. She might never again be asked to
head the department in his absence. She might even be demoted from her managerial position, perhaps even reduced
to the entry-level task of stocking the shelves.

She had taken a risk and gotten caught.

Jane had suspected that someone might file a protest. But
she had expected it to be with the store's illustrious owner,
Mr. Clark Baron. Jane had intended to call in Sir herself, once
the cash registers began to ring. She'd hoped he would come
down from his seventh-floor suite of offices to have a look at
her campaign, declare that this was just the sort of jolt his
antiquated Emporium needed. Congratulate her for showing him the light.

But there was no sign of the dashing silver-haired Sir. The
Emporium's toy department had been Nibling's kingdom for
the past three decades and he would be delivering his own
brand of restrained, shortsighted justice.

Nevertheless, the results of her display could not be de-
nied. Word had passed through the stuffy store like lightning. People were still flooding in to the department, crushing
closer for a good hard look at the play area. For years such
things as the castle, the lookout tower, the slide, the swing
and sandbox had been sold separately and discreetly from the
pages of a catalog at the counter.

This was a ground-breaking moment in Emporium history.

If only she'd managed to complete the sales before this confrontation. She couldn't bear to let one customer get away.

Nibling had managed to elbow his way through the crowd with his last ounce of aplomb. He stood at the bottom of the huge winding slide with his fists clenched at his sides and his egg-shaped face tight with suppressed rage.

The customers shot expectant looks at him, then sympathetic ones at her. A hush fell over the department, magnifying the classical background music.

Mozart, Nibling and the young female upstart who let the kids handle the toys. A pot that had been brewing for months.

"Miss Haley!" he bellowed with a sneeze and a wheeze. "What on earth have you done to my department?"

"Mister, uh, Nibling," she greeted perkily. "Shouldn't you be resting at home?"

"Indeed I should be! And would be, if it weren't for this contumacious stunt of yours."

"Sales are up this morning," she confided. As his mouth pruned, she realized this was the last thing he wanted to hear. He, of course, only wanted her to keep the status quo, not upstage him.

"This sort of frivolity is not on. Not in keeping with Baron's dignified quotidian."

A ripple of disappointment passed through the crowd, which, of course, made him all the angrier.

He shook a long bony finger in the air. "I demand you come down here at once!"

"Yes, of course." With a bright smile she launched herself forward into the deep, winding chute. It was anticlimactic to the finale she'd planned on the monkey bars, but it would have to do.

Nibling was waiting for her at the end of the line, and swiftly grasped her elbow as she popped to her feet. To all appearances, he was offering gallant assistance. In truth, he was immobilizing her. She tried to tug free of his grip only to feel his fingers pressing deeper into her arm.

"Don't even try to get away, Miss Haley," he cautioned softly with a false "floor" smile.

"But people are lining up at the counter," she protested.

"The others will handle the flow."

"But I should be in the lead!" she whispered back, her temper rising. "I deserve the biggest share of the customers . . . my commissions!"

He flashed a row of crowded teeth. "I think not."

"I think so! I went to a lot of trouble—"

"You've made a lot of trouble," he sharply reprimanded.

"But we're actually selling!" she sputtered, pointing to the row of people at the old wooden counter, filling out order forms for the Plas-Tek pieces.

He followed her gaze with a pained look. "I have neither the stamina nor the inclination to wait around while you attempt to profit from this spectacle."

"Then by all means, leave," she invited with innocent sweetness.

"Not until we put this before Sir," he clarified with a glint in his bleary eyes. "I insist you come along with me at once."

"Oh, all right. Let's get it over with." Jane wrenched free of his gnarly grip, adjusted her tutu, then accompanied him through the shoe department and the pharmacy to the bank of elevators near the front entrance.

Jane felt a painful stab of withdrawal as she moved farther and farther away from her customers. If only she'd had a chance to make her pitch to Clark Baron down here on the floor during this buying frenzy, shock him out of his outdated formalities. Seeing her plan in action might have been just the jolt he needed to rocket him straight from the fifties into the nineties.

Jane stepped into an elevator alongside Nibling, joining several customers already in the car. The Emporium was steeped in stiff-lipped service all the way, including operators in the ancient cages, who stopped on each of the six floors open to the public, announcing the departments at each and every stop.

Her mind ticked with possible comebacks to any and all lines tossed at her. She was humming with puissance by the time they marched down the old marble hallway on the private floor at the top. These offices bore far less traffic than the public ones below, evidenced by the high shine still on the rich mahogany and marble.

Despite the gleam, and the architectural splendor of the high ceilings, carved woodwork and ornate archways, this floor, like all the others, had a stifling aura, like that of a museum on the decline.

She had hoped to put a chink into this suffocating formality with her program downstairs. If only she could convince Sir that she had done well.

Mr. Baron's high-backed leather chair was facing the window overlooking the city street when his secretary ushered them in. One of the crank-out windows was open and downtown sounds drifted in on the spring breeze.

It wasn't like Sir to breath anything but antiquated air.

Which could mean this wasn't the Baron she was expecting.

Jane released a cry of indignation as the chair swiveled around. It just wasn't her day. First, cheated out of a gold mine of commissions and now . . . *him!*

Just as she feared, Gregory, looking smart and elegant in his custom double-breasted charcoal suit, was the Baron behind the massive old desk. The years had honed his striking features to a lean, hungry sharpness that made him all the more appealing to Jane. Even in his annoyed and impatient state, he was devastating.

Desmond Nibling inhaled, forcing a smile. "Mr. Baron, I—"

"You weren't expecting me," he interrupted in a brisk baritone.

"That is true," Nibling faltered. "A crisis which deserves Sir's immediate attention has arisen—"

"Well, Dad is under the weather today. He's home on doctor's orders."

"That is regrettable. You see—"

"Nibs, your problem precedes you," Greg swiftly interceded, shuffling aside some paperwork. "I know what happened down in Toys. And I believe we can handle it on our end without a lot of fuss."

"Of course," he intoned, working to conceal his doubt behind a blow into his snowy white handkerchief.

Greg's large mouth pulled tight. He could see the frustration on Nibs's pale blotchy face. Nibs didn't want to deal with the son. He wanted the king, the fossil. His father.

And it bothered the younger Baron a great deal. To all the employees of the Emporium, he was nothing more than Little Sir. Thirty pounds heavier and six inches taller than his father, and they referred to him as "little."

Caring at all was a damn stupid exercise and he knew it. He still had no desire to fill his father's shoes. At the age of forty, Greg was a success in his own right, a well-known producer of documentaries with a lavish list of credits. His programs ran the gamut from investigative to informative, airing on cable, public television and network prime time.

Greg was here to bail out his father, pure and simple. He'd temporarily set up an off-site branch of his company, Explore Unlimited, in the Barons' downtown St. Paul condo only blocks away from the store. There he could tend to his own business and be on call to fill in here at the store when Sir wasn't up to his duties.

This setup had been in operation since Christmastime, when Sir had had a heart attack. He'd lost Greg's mother, Amanda, last fall and was having a difficult time coping. The holiday had done him in. Greg had been visiting, and had made the decision to stay on indefinitely, flying back to Los Angeles on an intermittent basis.

Greg adored his father. Was sincerely grateful for the stable home life he provided him. Clark Baron was a family man all the way. Greg and his mother had been the center of his world.

Along with Mabel Haley, and her impish granddaughter, Jane.

Having no relatives of their own, they'd always been considered extended family. Greg had returned to the Twin Cities regularly over the years, seeking a relaxing counterpoint to his stressful fast-lane existence.

Janey had always welcomed him with open arms, proclaiming to be in dire need of tutorship in golf, tennis, volleyball—anything to garner his exclusive attention.

And he'd always come through.

There was no person on earth that he was closer to—or more unsure of.

Janey... A woman now, at twenty-five. Standing before him in a clingy lemon leotard and shimmery tights best suited for center ring under the big top. Steamed and outrageous and unpredictable.

She was fingering her tutu under his guarded gaze, just as she'd fingered her ruffled flower-girl dress so long ago. And those blue eyes were gleaming with an eerie light that made his gut flinch.

He hadn't seen that look in two decades.

Not since his wedding day.

The issue at hand obviously meant a lot to her. And she was primed to fight it with all she had.

"I would like a chance to explain why I did what I did," she blurted, pouncing closer to the desk.

Greg's eyes landed on her perky breasts, straining the Spandex confines of her suit. In a rash attempt to keep his wits and his distance, he leaned back in the huge springy chair, steepling his fingers beneath his chin. "Your intentions are obvious," he retorted impatiently.

She stiffened her spine under his long, dangerous look, cursing her bad luck of getting stuck with the wrong Baron. Sir was a gallant old softy when it came to the women in his life. He'd adored his late wife Amanda and had respected and sheltered her daffy Grandma Mabel, keeping her as his secretary when he could have found someone far more efficient to assist him. Jane might have had a chance of swaying Sir.

But Gregory Baron was a different mix. He could be difficult, distant, diffident—all at the same time if he wanted. And he wanted it right now, she inwardly fumed. He wouldn't be tolerant of any trouble concerning the department store, or concerning her. He was just riding things out now, until Sir could come back to work full-time, until he could run back to his California home. What a missed opportunity—with her and the store!

Oh, how she envied him his position at the helm of the Emporium. She'd love to have a hand at running the place, at bringing it back to its past glory.

"I wonder if perhaps your father would be up to taking a phone call," Nibling suggested in the silence.

Greg offered him a thin smile. "I think I can handle this, Nibs. It's just an isolated matter of policy—"

Nibling inhaled sharply. "This is an ongoing problem! Miss Haley is far too disruptive. Why, in a matter of a couple of days she coerced my entire staff into monkey outfits—"

"They are circus costumes," Jane objected with exasperation. "There aren't any animals, Gre—er, ah, Mr. Baron. Why, those outfits were put together with merchandise right here in the store!"

"That does not make them appropriate sales attire," Nibling retorted haughtily.

Gregory released a low, shuddering breath. Lord, she was lovely in that "inappropriate" sales attire, with her long black hair all wavy and wild. Just the sort of handful that could take up all of a man's time. Given the chance . . .

Since his return last December, he'd felt himself slipping slowly and languidly under her thumb. After spending the Yuletide together with his father and her grandmother, they'd just sort of drifted together into a very adult relationship. They hadn't dated each other exclusively at any point. Their hours were ones of quality rather than quantity.

Intense quality time summed it up perfectly.

He cleared his throat, wedging a finger into the crisp white collar of his shirt. Why was it suddenly so hard to swallow?

Perhaps it was because he could still so vividly picture Jane in his bed. Seductive, playful and generous in her lovemaking.

They'd crossed the carnal line back on Valentine's Day, after a pops concert at the Ordway and dinner at Fountaine's. They'd gone back to the Baron condo, full of laughter and expensive Chardonnay. It had been a delicious dessert.

And her idea, as he recalled.

But wasn't it always her way all the way?

The first time had been the hardest for him, fully accepting Jane as a sensual woman, old enough to handle no-strings pleasures. The intimate times to follow had been far easier for him, in a shamelessly habit-forming way. He'd grown so shameless, in fact, that he'd done what he deemed the right thing a couple of weeks ago, he'd broken up with her for good.

Nibling was ranting on in his hoity-toity tone during Greg's reflective pause, as agitated as he'd ever seen him. "One single morning, Mr. Baron, and this teasing—"

"I didn't tease him!" Jane cried out in defense.

Not on purpose, anyway, Greg inwardly lamented. But what man wasn't rattled by her impetuous charms? After months of working side by side with the staid old Nibs, it was surprising that a clash of this sort hadn't happened a whole lot sooner. Nibling was a hands-off man and she was a hands-on woman.

Hands-on. And a handful, too.

The line between his brows deepened as he scowled in frustration. This pair would manage to erupt on a day when Sir was recharging his batteries. As usual, Greg was merely on hand to baby-sit, to enforce his father's outdated rules on formal sales techniques. He tried not to dwell on the fact that he'd found sales to be at an all-time low. And that his crafty old dad clutched his chest with suspect pain the few times Greg had tried to talk to him about it.

At this frustrating point, Greg felt obligated to reflect only his father's wishes. Nibling would be Sir's first concern. Nibling and tradition.

No matter that Jane's eyes could rival the clear blue waters of St. Thomas. That her nose turned up in the cutest way and that her mouth was always so kissably lush. Or that she was wearing a sinfully expensive scent that she sprayed on each and every morning at the perfume-sampling counter.

Greg gave his blond head a clearing shake. This was no time to dwell on the personal.

This was a conflict concerning departmental policy.

One Jane was going to lose. One she would make personal enough for both of them!

"I'd never pester him," she was raving on in disgust. "Why, that's unthinkable. Unbelievable."

"That'll do, Miss Haley," Greg interjected as Nibling reddened to his thinning hairline.

"I've had carte blanche in Toys since the moon landing," Nibling lectured, hooking his fingers in his belt loops. "And I will not have anyone disrupting my well-oiled machine."

"Your gears are rusty," Jane declared. "It's time for new direction, innovative sales techniques." She whirled back to Greg. "You know what I'm talking about. What better way to motivate sales than through visualization, demonstration? I say quality merchandise should be shown off!"

"Romping around in a tacky costume is not dignified under any circumstances," Nibling sputtered in horror.

She leveled an accusing finger at him. "You stole away my dignity when you hauled me to my feet and pried me away from all those customers! I'm walking out of here with no respect and no commission!"

"What makes you think you're walking out of here with your job?" Nibling inquired loftily.

She gasped in dismay. "I didn't think—"

"Indeed you did not!"

"Slow down, Desmond," Greg cautioned, raising a hand.

"I shall do no such thing," he snapped. "This girl is out. *O-u-t.*"

"Fired for increasing Baron's sales?" she squawked in disbelief.

"I shan't work with her another minute," Nibling threatened. "And if you can't clear her out of my hair—"

"You haven't had real hair in twenty years, according to Mabel," Jane hooted, her patience snapping. She faced Greg squarely, her hands at her hips. "Can you honestly tell me that the Baron family would rather retain their stuffy traditions than earn an extra buck?"

Greg met her burning stare with irritation and begrudging admiration, fervently wishing he was halfway across the world doing what he loved best, filming a documentary on some war-torn country or the Amazon rain forest.

He cleared his throat, looking for the proper words. "Speaking for my father—"

"Who would want what's best for me," she lashed back.

"Who would put the Emporium first," he corrected.

"Get on with it, man!" Nibling blustered. "I have a department to straighten out!"

"Then go ahead and take care of it," Greg directed, gesturing toward the frosted-glass door.

Nibling stared at him for a long, uncertain moment. "Very well. I know I can trust you to serve our best interests, keep your father calm and satisfied." With that loaded message to the younger Baron, he turned to Jane, bowing slightly with a mocking gleam in his eye. "Goodbye, Miss Haley. I will have a stock boy collect any personal belongings you may have left in my domain and have them sent up here directly."

Once Nibling whisked the door shut after himself, Jane whirled back on Greg. "Are you going to let him do this to me?"

"You had to know you were taking a risk."

"You know all about risks!" she asserted in wheedling accusation. "You take them all the time in your work!"

He shrugged in concession. "You've set yourself up in a structured arena where change is nonexistent."

"Change would be the best thing that ever happened to that department—the whole damn store," she declared, rapping her knuckles on the polished desktop for effect.

"That isn't for you to decide."

"But I know—"

"Maybe that's your trouble," he complained. "You're never satisfied with being a part of the show. You expect to be the center attraction!"

Jane sidled up to the desk and pressed her hands on his outdated blotter, bringing her face down within inches of his. "I was too much for you, wasn't I? I thought that might be the case."

He blinked into her blue eyes, full of mocking fury. "I'd rather not bring our relationship into this."

"You'd rather we not've had one in the first place!" She leaned even closer, brushing her small upturned nose against his. "But we did. *Do it*, I mean. And now you want me out of the way. I think you've just been waiting for an excuse to toss me aside."

"Not so," he objected fiercely, pinching her chin in his fingers.

"We were fine until we had sex, Greg."

"The sex was just fine, Jane."

"But it made you nervous, didn't it?" she accused, lurching out of his reach. "You felt your freedom was in jeopardy. You could feel your license to prowl slipping away."

"That's nuts. I'm trying to behave like a responsible adult, not some kind of randy predator!" When she averted her eyes with a sniff of doubt, he went on to state his case calmly but firmly. "We parted ways for good for some very solid reasons. At twenty-five you're looking for a family man. At forty, I feel like that role has passed me by. I like my life as it is, honey. It's damn near perfect."

She turned back, forcing an audacious smile. "Maybe I won't need babies."

"You will," he said with quiet confidence. "We went over all of this very rationally, came to mutual—"

"I remember you using words like *difficult, petulant*," she recollected poutily.

"I was angry. We were having one of our little tiffs, remember?"

"Lively discussions!" she protested.

His face smoldered. "When you're forty, they are unnecessary, aggravating tiffs, Janey!"

She folded her arms across her chest. "You'd just like to see me vanish. I know I'm right."

"You've been a part of my life since you could walk," he growled in objection. "Hell, I know better than to ever imagine life without you."

"Know better?" she gasped in mortification. "Thanks a heap!"

"You're twisting my meaning," he gently accused. "I'm merely saying that, odds are, we'll always be close in some form. Our families have deep ties." He sighed under her penetrating gaze. "I don't mean to give you a hard time. I am the temporary one here."

That fact secretly hurt her the most. No matter how she'd tried over the past few months to be irresistible and indispensable, Greg just couldn't see it. Her dream of them one day running the Emporium as a team was finally biting the dust for good. He had a whole other life waiting for him back in California. A life that even included his ex-wife Nicole, who still worked for his production company. He could work with her. Even after their embarrassingly short six-month marriage.

Greg felt a stab of remorse as her face crumpled over her secret musings.

"If it's any consolation, I understand what you were trying to do in Toys." When her thin black brows arched in hope, he swiftly went on in clarification. "But believe me, Sir is a grouchy gramps when it comes to tradition. He would never forgive me if we revamped this tomb without his okay. It could lead to another heart attack, which is just what we're all hoping to avoid, right?"

She nodded. "Of course. I just thought that coming from me, with Nibling out of the way... Well, I hoped he might see a glimmer of light."

"He might have," Greg conceded. "He's always spoiled you rotten."

Always hoped you and I would connect in these later years, he added silently. But he kept that nugget of truth to himself. Jane didn't need further encouragement!

"So you're not going to fire me, then?" she demanded fretfully.

"No, no, of course not! Sir wouldn't want you out."

She watched his features tighten with his words. He hated like hell acting for any other man. It went against his grain. His philosophies were different from his father's, but they shared the same backbone, the same drive.

It was no wonder that he was torn between two worlds. He wanted to please his father, but he wanted to live his own life.

And in the center of it all, she wanted him.

Jane's own desperate feelings of love had lingered on through the years beyond his wedding, blossoming into something lasting and meaningful. Now, after she'd given herself to him, she could feel him slipping through her fingers. Sir was putting in more store hours now, and Greg was preparing to retreat to his wonderful world where all his dreams had supposedly been realized.

For a man who claimed his world was damn near perfect, he certainly seemed to be kicking up a hell of a commotion!

The air was crackling with electricity right up to the ceiling fan spinning sixteen feet above them. Greg was motionless, clenching the arms of his huge chair.

The next move was hers.

She sank her teeth into her red lip as she regarded him with a mixture of exasperation and grief. If she could just somehow regain Greg's affections and her position in Toys. Maybe if she appealed to his ego, he just might override Nibling's wishes and send her back to her old job. Tradition be damned!

"Sir's wants, Sir's expectations," she taunted sweetly. "Is that all you really want out of this post?"

He crooked his finger at her, beckoning her closer to the desk. She glided forward with a ballerina's grace worthy of her outfit, tipping close for a show of cleavage.

"You know what I really want?" he crooned.

She smiled with a breathless sigh. "What?"

"Peace," he declared flatly. "So stop trying to jerk me around!"

She could have slapped away his superior smile, but that was just the legitimate reason he needed to dismiss her.

She moved out of smacking range for her own good, pacing the length of the huge shiny desk. His eyes were trained on her legs, burning holes through her glossy stockings. Finally! A weakness!

"For a man of peace, you sure have some antsy ideas," she lilted knowingly.

He rubbed his chin in bemusement. "Huh?"

"You just can't stop giving me a second look even now, can you?" she accused with a blurt of laughter. "Can't stop imagining what I look like underneath—"

"I'm not doing that!"

"Sure you are!" she announced grandly, tossing her wavy raven hair over her shoulder. "You can't control yourself."

He made a strangled noise. "This is a business meeting. I am supposed to look at you."

"Above the tutu, would seem more sincere."

She had him dead right. They both knew it as his eyes snapped up to her face.

With a growl he swiveled his chair back toward the open window. "Hell, maybe I should just fire you!"

"It's all so disconcerting," she taunted with mock despair, rounding the desk in pursuit. "Considering that when you stare at me, you really do know what I look like without my clothes on. It isn't just a fanciful estimation that the average boss might make in a naughty moment. I mean, you really do know. For sure." She sagged back against the windowsill as if drained.

"And you know what I look like!" he retorted. "So we're even."

With a provocative flutter of lashes she studied his body in the roomy leather chair.

He shifted in discomfort under her bold scrutiny. "What are you doing?"

"Trying to remember," she breathed with a maddening smile. "Just to keep things fair, of course."

"Well, cut it out and listen to me," he ordered. "I can't let you go back down to Nibling's department."

"But I love my job," she wailed in dismay. "The customers, the toys, the challenge to make the next sale!"

"I understand that. I admire that."

She clasped her hands together in prayer. "Give it back to me, Greg. Please."

"I can't."

"I belong in Toys," she babbled on. "I've been patiently biding my time down there, just waiting for old Nibling to hobble off into retirement. It's my rightful place!"

She searched his silver-gray gaze for some understanding. Much of what she said about biding her time and wanting her rightful place fit their relationship, as well. Couldn't he see how ideal their setup had been? Didn't he have any soul-searing regrets?

"Dad can't let Nibling down," he strained to explain. "They're like two old warriors."

"He wouldn't want my toes tromped on, either!" she scoffed.

"A minute ago you were relieved that I wasn't going to fire you," he blurted out in frustration.

"Well, it isn't enough," she claimed with a dismissive gesture.

Which was a big part of the reason why Greg just couldn't find a compatible middle ground with Jane. She demanded so much of him, so much time. Expected him to flex with every whim.

Unlike many of his counterparts, he enjoyed women his own age. They were often set in their ways, often shared his love of film, and always knew better than to twist him in knots just for fun.

They were . . . comfortable. They understood about personal space and private downtime, respected his need to unwind after a heavy assignment.

"I truly believe that Sir could be brought around to some modern ideas with just the right push," she was insisting with a stubborn lift of her chin.

"Maybe so," Greg conceded. "But timing and restraint aren't your specialities. You never look before you leap."

"I'm looking now. . . ." With a sultry murmur she eased up from the sill and into his lap. She drew a polished fingernail along with jawline, plowing through his five o'clock shadow. It made an audible scratching sound—of promise.

A shudder shook him. Now who was getting personal! But a little hypocrisy wasn't about to keep Janey from a goal. The single scratch was licking through his insides like liquid fire now. Her touch did that to him. Despite the rational reasons for their breakup, she was the ultimate sex kitten. And cuddling in his lap this way was the worst kind of temptation. He fought the surge of energy centering in his groin, focusing on her manipulative ploy with every ounce of objectivity he possessed.

This was a last-ditch effort. Which was going to get her nowhere.

"I'm sure you'll have another shot at Sir, Jane," he said with deliberate modulation. "With proper rest, a healthier diet, and some duty delegation to trusted store personnel, he will most likely run this seven-story museum for at least another decade."

"Oh." Her face fell. Her last weapon, her best weapon had failed.

With a wistful look she fingered the hair dusting his collar. Ironically, it was again styled in the careless, bleached shag of his first, wedding-day rejection.

"Jane, I—"

She pressed her fingers to his mouth, easily reading the no-go in his granite features. "Save it. I'm out of Toys. But just what are you going to do with me?"

Bracing himself, he told her.

2

"I KNOW YOU'RE NOT expecting me, Grandma."

"Janey, dear!" Mabel lilted in surprise. "Come right in, of course!"

It was six o'clock that evening, an hour after Baron's closing time. Jane was at Mabel Haley's door in the navy suit she'd worn to work that day, her leotard and tutu tucked away in the roomy white tote bag slung over her shoulder. After her grueling afternoon, she was in dire need of a sympathetic ear and had automatically come running to the only mother she'd ever known, her grandmother.

Mabel was, of course, in the perfect position to understand Jane's quandary, having served as Sir's private secretary for years. At seventy-two, she'd long since retired and moved into a St. Paul high rise full of older people in similar circumstances. She enjoyed her cards and knitting and community-service tasks. But she still was a Baron employee by proxy. She lived for tales of the store.

Jane scooted into the entryway, dabbing her red-rimmed eyes with the damp tissue knotted in her hand. She paused to look at Mabel for the first time, and realized that she was in the midst of either coming or going. There was a round blue straw hat with a single feather set atop her neat white curls, rouge on her chipmunk cheeks, and her rounded figure was on display in one of Baron's mid-priced floral-print jerseys.

"Maybe this isn't the best time, Gran," she croaked in lame apology.

"Don't be ridiculous, dear." With the motions of a plump mother hen she ushered Jane inside, steering her into the small cozy living room stuffed with dark Victorian furniture more suited to Mabel's old house in Highland Park. Jane had confided many a dilemma to her on the very velvet-covered sofa they were sinking onto now. Many of Jane's schoolgirl friends had occupied these cushions as well, way back when, for a dose of Mabel's nonjudgmental advice. Mabel was the only bohemian their old neighborhood had ever known. An avid listener and an entertaining counselor, she was a natural for confidences.

And the fact that she would inevitably get all the facts in a muddle soon thereafter made her a good security risk.

"Have plans for tonight?" Jane asked in contrite panic.

"No, thank you, dear," Mabel declined, misinterpreting Jane's words. "Just got back from a lovely lunch, though. Of course we ate late in the afternoon, so one might consider it an early supper. What would one call that, Janey?"

"As long as you're not hungry, it doesn't matter, Mabbe."

"Are you hungry?" Mabel inquired with probing solicitousness. "I have a chicken leg left over from last night that I was going to eat if I hadn't eaten so late this afternoon."

She forced a bleary smile. "Not right now."

"Of course, you want to talk first," she amended with sympathetic realization as she scanned Jane's pale, tear-stained features. "I see that your plan of revamping Baron's has left you in tears."

"It has not!" Jane's back stiffened.

"'Twas a gamble." Mabel picked up a crotchet-covered tissue box from the coffee table and set it in Jane's lap.

Jane pulled forth a fresh tissue to accommodate her drippy nose. "You don't understand," she managed to croak through her closing throat. "I'm not crying."

Mabel tsked with concern. "Then you've caught Nibling's cold."

"I'd never get that close to him," she spat with a cringe.

"Then what on earth . . . ?"

"Well, to begin with. I've—" Jane tried to spit out the horrid truth, choking on the words. "Been banished. Banished to the Bargain Basement!"

Mabel swallowed the news like a vial of hemlock. "That would have set me to tears, as well."

Jane shook her head forcefully. "It's my allergies. They're raging. Do you know how many separate scents there are on the notions counter down there?"

"There used to be twenty-seven kinds of scent," Mabel automatically clarified. She might not remember her grocery list, but Mabel had a virtual library of Baron's facts and figures stored away in her brain.

"There are now double that amount!" Jane plucked a fresh tissue from the box and waved it around. "What with all the gimmicky soaps and bubble baths and assorted things that never used to need a smell to work. Crayons, paper, hair bows... They all stink to high heaven! And they're all in that wretched department."

"Wonder what particular vermin got up your nose," Mabel clucked.

"Nibling was the first," she sputtered, her voice gaining strength. "He rushed in to spoil my whole presentation of the Plas-Tek equipment. Then he brought me directly up to the seventh-floor offices for a quick trial and immediate sentencing. I lost my commissions and my spot in Toys."

"I can't believe Sir would do such a thing," Mabel declared in affronted surprise.

"*Greg* did it!" she cried out in enraged disbelief. "Claimed it was on his father's behalf. The nerve!"

Mabel's fingers flew to her doughy cheek. "Oh? Oh, my."

"I thought he was going to fire me at first. Nibs wanted him to." She sighed hard. "Greg just didn't seem to know what to do with me."

"I dare say he never did," Mabel lilted with twinkling eyes.

"I had the feeling that he would've liked to give me the boot—"

"Oh, Janey! No!"

Jane held her chin high, her moist eyes squinting meanly. "He just didn't have the guts."

"He seems more than capable of doing exactly as he pleases," Mabel protested. "A man who has taken pictures of naked natives in the deepest of Africa." Her eyes widened as she envisioned what sort of courage and daring filming such a documentary would take.

"Well, I had all afternoon to think about why he didn't give me the chop. Think and gag and sniffle. Maybe he's trying to avoid giving me severance pay. If I quit, the store wouldn't owe me a cent."

Mabel pursed her lips. "That's nonsense. The Barons have been so generous with us over the years. Treated us like family!"

"Or maybe he was afraid I'd make an scene. If he'd thrown me out on my tutu, there would have automatically been some speculation in the departments. It would've aimed a spotlight on our unbusinesslike relationship! Every starry-eyed shopgirl would suddenly see the barrier between the classes as penetrable."

Jane liked the feel of that conclusion. Greg was afraid she'd kiss and tell. That would be a nightmare to both Baron men. They preferred to keep their distance from the employees and their personal affairs private.

Jane and Mabel had always been the exception to that rule. No doubt, because, unlike the Barons, the Haleys hated rules of all kinds and blithely ignored them whenever possible.

Their intermingling roles as employees and surrogate family members made for complicated dynamics. They were far too close to be considered outsiders. But at the same time they were obligated to adhere to the basic Emporium policies.

Firing Jane would have been taking a tremendous risk. She might have blown the lid off!

"They had earrings in many parts of their bodies, you know," Mabel reflected with a measure of horrified delight.

Jane blinked. "Who? What?"

"The natives, dear. Aren't you listening? Of course I imagine if a ring is attached to another part of one's anatomy, one couldn't very well call it an earring. Belly button ring, nose ring, nipple ring. Now, pinkie rings are a whole other kettle of fish, my girl!"

Jane sighed in loving exasperation, more than accustomed to her aunt's sporadic flights into fancy. "We're talking about my demotion," she patiently redirected.

Mabel tossed back her fluffy white head, causing the tall blue feather in her hat to waggle. "Yes, indeed. But piercing one's flesh," she intimated on a low confidential note, "especially in tender areas, is a difficult issue to ignore. Must be quite painful."

Jane watched her grandma cringe in the throes of creative visualization. Haleys never liked to miss a sensation or an opportunity. But Jane had no time for these delays.

"What's Greg trying to do to me, Mabbe?"

Mabel's eyes popped back open. "I imagine he's just trying to represent his father the best way he can," she hazarded to guess.

"He didn't bother to check with Sir, though, did he? Run his torture-of-choice by him?"

"I will call Sir myself," Mabel announced with resolve. "Right this instant."

Jane caught her soft fleshy arm, pulling Mabel back beside her on the the sofa. "No, no, I want to handle this myself."

Mabel sighed. "There must be a compromise. Another open position in another department. Perhaps if you spoke to Gregory about that option."

"I did. His excuse was that the openings in the plum commission departments are few and far between. Due to the recession, they have an overload of overly qualified employees. An avalanche of applications. The store is apparently full of rocket scientists and philosophers. With professors and brain surgeons waiting in the wings."

Mabel raised a finger in objection. "Ah, but you are a specialist at Baron's. A professional salesperson with a line of patter so sweet as to charm the very birds from the trees."

"Yes, you're right," Jane agreed with renewed fortitude. Her qualities and options were clearer now that both her symptoms and temper were ebbing into a comfort zone. "I'll just have to fight for a fair deal. But I can't afford to do too much time down in the bargain basement. I wouldn't last a week, what with a bloated face, red itchy eyes, and a nose dripping like a leaky faucet."

Mabel squeezed Jane's hand with her plump one. "We must take care of you. Of course we must."

They sat silently for a few moments, lost in thought.

"Let's try to appeal to Gregory once more," Mabel suggested hopefully. "While you're still aflame with your symptoms."

"Why do you keep going back to him!" Jane objected with an indignant sniff.

"Because I think he should have a chance to see your suffering, to make this right of his own accord."

"Well, I did try to give him another chance. I raced back up there on my afternoon break, and he was already gone for the weekend! Off to Los Angeles to tend to his own affairs. One of the office underlings with no real power and no real interest was at his desk."

"Oh, my. He really doesn't want to lose hold of that other job of his, does he?" Mabel fretted.

"No! And you and Sir can just forget about him staying on here permanently. He can't wait to go back to his old life."

Mabel's expression clouded, but she was silent.

"Let's send Sir a letter," Jane decided, "to his North Oaks estate. I'll outline the facts in black-and-white. He can study them. Be the judge of my fate."

Mabel nodded. "Yes, that may be our only option left."

"You'll type it, won't you?"

"Yes, of course," Mabel purred confidently. "Easy as rolling around on a log."

With Mabel in the lead they marched into her small sitting room behind the kitchen. Mabel sat down at her old rolltop before her ancient Remington manual typewriter. She began to organize herself, peeling the dustcover off the machine, rummaging through a drawer for a sheet of white paper. Jane roamed around the cluttered room, watching Mabel assume the position at the typewriter that she'd honed to perfection as Sir's private secretary. Her spine was stiff, her fingers were arched over the home-row keys. Even the single feather in her straw hat was at full attention.

It was clear that Mabel was excited about getting behind a desk again to prepare this simple business letter. But in her own words, it was bound to be on a par with "rolling around on a log." Mabel's letters tended to drift in the same manner her conversations did. Jane would have to watch over her closely.

"Let's start with the date," Jane suggested.

"What date? You have a date? With who? Gregory?"

"The date," she reiterated, moving over to the desk. "March thirty-first."

"Oh, yes. Certainly." Mabel pecked at the stiff keys with high-jumping fingers. "I'll put your name and address on top, too."

Jane patiently waited as Mabel made the additions. "Okay. Let's go on with, 'Dear Sir.' Or shall we say, poor gramps, naive soul . . . ?"

"'Sir' sounds like the best beginning," Mabel mused. "Don't you think so, dear? I agree that those other things you said about Sir may be true, Jane, but—"

"That naive stuff was nothing for the letter, Gran," she patiently corrected. "I was just spouting off about how Greg seems to be leading Sir around by a ring in his nose."

"Not rings again!" Mabel huffed with exasperation. "Could this be a pattern with Gregory? Filming these rings in Africa, now pressing one on Sir, pulling him around by it?"

"I just feel that Sir would've handled the situation more objectively," Jane sought to explain. "Of course Greg claimed to be acting on Sir's behalf. But I think he's most interested in getting me out of the way. The basement is the bottom, after all."

"Clark wouldn't approve," Mabel concurred.

"Well, this is our chance to let him know how things are done in his absence. Let's make this letter good."

Mabel took a deep breath. "Very well."

Jane squinted in thought. "Type this.

"I was so sorry to discover that you weren't up to being in the office today. I was very anxious to speak to you on an urgent matter concerning sales technique. Instead, I was forced to speak with your egotistical, bull-headed, unfeeling—"

"Son," Mabel condensed in a chirp. "Speak with your s-o-n."

Jane frowned over the edit, but continued.

"As you no doubt know by now, I have been demoted to the Bargain Basement. I feel this downgrading is directly connected to my breakup with Greg. It's obvious that he transferred me to the basement to get me out of the way. I don't know if he's coercing me to quit, or if he just figures that putting me in the bowels of the building will limit our contact. In any case, I don't think it's fair that I be punished over our failed love affair."

Mabel absorbed that statement with a scrunched brow, then verbalized her own translation. "Finding myself no longer on Gregory's arm, I feel that . . ."

Jane moved up behind Mabel to monitor her progress, biting back an involuntary grin. Her grandmother had the gist of her message intact so far. But Jane hadn't been positioned exactly on Greg's arm during their happiest moments. She thought the expression seemed dated and told her so.

"Trouble with dates again," Mabel lamented.

Jane removed her grandma's feathered hat, patting her fluff of hair. "Never mind."

Mabel typed on with a sure smile. "The right phrasing is important. Sir has always been fond of formal terms and will appreciate your message all the more. You wouldn't believe the pains he and I took with each and every letter that left his office. It felt like nothing ever slipped out without his okay."

"Ah, but that's because you were always too carefree to be trusted," Jane teased, gently placing her aunt's hat on the cluttered sewing table.

Mabel slanted her a sly smile, shaving a couple of decades off her seventy-two years. "Well . . . His old-world manner

made it easier not to fall in love with him while he and
Amanda were married. I cherished her friendship more than
life itself."

Jane nodded in understanding. "Let's continue.

"I'm sure my sales experiment with Plas-Tek toys has
reached your ears, as well. I did it for the good of Baron's! I expected a reward for my efforts, not a punish-
ment! At the very least, I would like the compensation
due me. The sales generated by my presentation had to
bring in sizable commissions."

Jane paused as Mabel worked to catch up, then continued
slowly.

"I wouldn't mind a transfer to another department offering as many opportunities as Toys. In any case, I
cannot tolerate an extended stay in Bargain Basement
Notions. Due to my allergies, the situation is intolera-
ble. A single afternoon among all the different scents,
and my head is spinning. My eyes are teary, my face
bloated, and I am exhausted from head to toe.
    "I am bringing my case to you as a last resort. I know
how much faith you have in Greg. Until now, I shared
that faith. But he is directly responsible for my condition and behaving impossibly! He has me trapped, holds
my future in his hands! Please don't let him ruin me."

Mabel pursed her plum-colored lips as she scanned the
sheet. "You don't feel that you're being a bit hard on Gregory, do you? This may spoil your chances of ever getting back
on his arm—so to speak."

"My job holds far more promise than he does."

"If you were to try to appeal to him again first thing Monday..."

Jane reared back in affront. "No way! He had his opportunity. Instead of showing me an ounce of understanding, of dividing the blame between Nibling and me, he chose the coward's way out!"

Mabel gaped. "He's not a coward. He's wrestled alligators!"

"Too bad they didn't take a little nip out of his tough hide."

"Janey, dear! I can't put that in the letter!"

"I don't want you to," she hastily assured. "All we need now is a closing."

Mabel responded with a tap-tap-tap.

Jane sidled up behind her for a final peek. "Looks pretty good," she judged, with a pat to her grandmother's shoulder.

"Hmm, yes. One more run-through should make it perfect."

"Looks fine, really."

Mabel leaned back in her chair and squinted at the paper. "I can do better. And I so want Clark to know that I've still got it."

Jane laughed in spite of her inflamed temper. "All right. But it's my guess that Sir knows exactly what you're made of already."

Mabel's pleading look grew solicitous as she eyed her granddaughter. "Are you feeling all right?"

Jane shrugged, leaning against the bookcase near the door. "I do feel a bit ragged," she admitted. "Guess I've reached my limit."

"Go and make us a cup of tea," Mabel directed with a shooing motion.

"You might need me for editing—"

"I am quite capable of handling this project," Mabel insisted as she reached for a fresh sheet of paper.

"If you don't mind, I think I'll rustle up some dinner, too," Jane said, moving to the door with a rub to her hollow stomach.

"I knew you were starving the moment you walked in the door," Mabel declared matter-of-factly. "You just needed time to realize it."

She was right! Jane wasn't sure how her flighty grandma could make such insightful observations out of the clear blue. But Mabel herself was first to admit that it was her keen sensibilities rather than any knack for practicalities, that always had gotten her by.

Jane ate a hearty meal of leftover chicken, mashed potatoes and corn, then dozed off on the old velvet sofa to the twitter of a Friday-night sitcom. When she awoke, it was nearly eight-thirty. Mabel was busily knitting in a nearby recliner.

Jane watched her yank and weave the soft variegated yarn around small metal needles. She'd grown up to that comforting click, click, click and it always made her feel warm and wanted.

"Like it so far?" Mabel asked cheerily, holding up the meager beginnings of a small pastel baby afghan. "Just had the urge to start it tonight."

"Is that for one of the charities?" Jane asked over the throes of a yawn.

"It's for whomever is in need, as always," she chirped. "I like these tight infant weaves so. It's important not to use a pattern with holes. Babies drag their blankets everywhere once they begin to toddle and always get their chubby fingers caught in the looser weaves." She held up her handiwork. "Now you can see that this weave has no 'loopholes' at all."

"It's quite nice." Visions of her own comfy bed, empty and waiting in her suburban Woodbury apartment urged Jane to her feet. "Guess I'll be running along."

Mabel nodded and smiled. "All right, dear. Unless you'd care to spend the night right here."

"No, I'll just take the letter and go." Jane rose to her feet and scanned all the coffee tables and the mantel for a sign of it.

"Edith Ginty down the hall could tell you all about it," Mabel reported dourly.

"My letter?"

"No, no," Mabel scoffed. "Keep up. Her eighteen-month-old grandson got his finger caught in a holey afghan. It was swollen purple before the little mite made a squeak. Edith had to cut it. Not the finger, of course. But the afghan itself. She was sick. The yarn was high-grade."

"Where is the letter?" Jane persisted.

Mabel tsked with a dismissive sweep her of hand. "I posted it long ago, in the box down the street. There is a late pickup on weeknights, so it will be in Sir's hands sometime tomorrow."

Jane's smile froze on her face. "So you think you got everything down pat, then?"

"Certainly, Janey," she assured with a click of her needles. "Straightforward situation, really. The facts are clearly plain to see. Like rolling around on a log."

3

UNLIKE JANE, GREG HAD no one to rouse him from his Friday-evening snooze on a sofa. He spent the entire night on a green leather one in his production office clear across the country. Explore Unlimited was located in California's exclusive Brentwood community, in a small office park of white plaster buildings nestled among palms and rich red begonias. The building had been his graduation gift from Sir. Greg had suspected at the time that it was more a consolation prize, an indirect reward for divorcing rough-edged Nicole—a woman who, Sir was certain, would never give Greg a secure home-life and a parcel of robust children.

It had annoyed Greg then, but the passing of two decades had healed all the old war wounds of his youth. The building had more than tripled in value. And he and Nicole had found they could continue working together in harmony, with each other and their college pal Kevin Cross. She still shared part of the dream they'd envisioned on their wedding day—the production company, and all the interesting adventures that went along with documenting slices of life on film.

Despite the collapse of their marriage, their faded infatuation, Nicole had proven determined to forge a lesser relationship with Greg, keeping her assistant producer's position in the company and the Baron name. Greg had no reason to deny her these things. She was efficient in her job and had never interfered with his life-style. It was a dead-end relationship of convenience, one that neither of them had bothered to reevaluate in a good long while.

It was his ex-wife who was now shaking him awake, with a none-too-gentle jostle.

"Rise and shine, Baron!"

Greg groaned and stiffened, his legs falling off the confines of the boxy couch. He'd been ignoring her for several minutes, lost in limbo between his two worlds where no one could touch him. He reluctantly opened his eyes, wincing against the brilliance of the sun-splashed room. As the Emporium was Midwestern conservatism with its dark woods and pinkish marble, his bungalow-style office was stark-white stucco and windowpanes, with lots of living plants adding a dash of West Coast green.

He always found it easier to think here, away from family pressures. As much as he would like to set them all aside, he knew it would be wise to take some downtime today, examine the situation with Jane and Clark and the store at a safe, more comfortable distance.

But Nicole would have to come first, for it was her long tanned body presently hovering over his, her strong hands clamped to his shoulders.

"I'm with it," he grumbled, sitting up to evade her grasp. "Just need a minute..."

"Okay, okay." She straightened in surrender but stayed in his line of vision. As par for the office, she was dressed in earth-toned clothing with simple lines. It was all part of her strong personality. With her hair dyed a bright yellow and clipped close to her head, her strong features void of any feminine paint, she made a forceful figure.

There was nothing wrong with her stark look, or her plain, practical attitude. It just didn't set his heart to beating anymore, as it had in his serious, save-the-world stage.

Now, dainty little Janey made him dance inside.

Lithe and electric in an exciting way. Yet somehow fragile, to ensure getting her own way. She had him on a roller-coaster ride of bewilderment and frustration. He went from glorying in her ambitious outlook, to blowing his top over her stubbornness and faith in happy endings for everyone.

He wished he could just get a look inside her head. Figure out what made her tick. But, hell, he knew no man would ever get in there. Not without marrying her, anyway.

Yeah, she'd let her husband in there, he decided with a sure nod of his head. She'd coyly held that apple out in temptation, along with all the other assets she had to offer.

She'd let him inside her body, but made it clear that that wasn't the best place to be. That entrée to her heart was the ultimate prize.

How damn clever, for a woman her age!

Ultimately it was another form of control, tied up in a prettier package. A small, tight, irresistible package full of surprises and delights.

But the price tag on the package was too high for a man who'd already been through life's grinder more times than he could count. It was the sort of challenge young idealists shot for.

Greg groaned, rubbing his suntanned temples. He couldn't give her what she needed. A beginning, a future full of promise. He'd somehow missed the family detour along the way, avoiding remarriage for nineteen years. He was old and cynical, with not a trace of shine left on him.

She was on the other side of the rainbow, still believing a pot of gold awaited her.

"Greg, Greg, you know better than to bunk down on this thing," Nicole was scolding through his musings. "At your age, with your back."

"It is a Hide-A-Bed sofa," he protested with a huge bear-like yawn.

"But the bed's still in hiding," she mocked, folding her arms across her chest.

He ran a hand through his shaggy blond hair and gazed down at his rumpled blue T-shirt and demin cutoffs. "I meant to zip back to my house for some real rest. Must've drifted off reading . . ."

Nicole huffed in disgust as she reached to pick up the bound manuscript from the tiled floor. "You were reading the script for the British special. Did it really put you to sleep?"

Greg stood with a mighty stretch. "Well, it isn't at all what I'm looking for. You know that."

"But I just thought that if you saw the concept on paper—" She broke off with a frustrated wave. "I think this writer captures the dignity of the country—"

"Nik . . ." Greg regarded her with a wry look.

She sighed. "You know I wrote it, don't you!"

His eyes crinkled at the corners. "After all our years together, I would recognize your voice anywhere. And it was silly to try and throw a blind piece at me, just to test my objectivity."

"Well, since you've been jockeying back and forth between here and your hometown, I feel as though I'm in a tug-of-war with your father."

"You have no reason to feel threatened by *Jane*," he corrected. "Isn't that who you've been building up a steam over since Christmas?"

"Well, can you blame me for wondering about her?" Nicole challenged with unusual emotion. "She put a curse on our wedding, didn't she? And it failed within six short months! I don't want her putting a curse on our business affairs, too!"

"She was a kid in kindergarten back then!"

"She isn't a kid anymore. I mean, we've had such a nice professional setup here since college, with you producing, Kevin directing, and me doing everything else. Relationships like ours take years to hone. It works so well between the three of us, dammit!"

"Are you talking business or romance?" he challenged.

"I just feel that this could be the end of us, with this whole alternate life-style waiting back there for you," she replied evasively, crossing the room to fiddle with the pale wooden miniblinds on the window facing the parking lot.

Greg's golden brows narrowed as he scanned the length of her sturdy back. "You've become way too focused on my personal affairs. This territorial turn isn't like you."

"Territorial?" she repeated hotly.

"Don't lie to yourself of all people," he admonished with a shake of his head.

All these years since the divorce, Greg would have sworn up and down that Nicole had not an ounce of real feeling left for him. But this little scene had been coming on for months, ever since he'd begun his commuting schedule.

And she had no right to put him on the spot.

Yes, they had shared a sexual intimacy on occasion—as some divorced couples were known to do. But the traces of puppy love that had brought them together in the first place had long since died, leaving them both on the lookout for something more satisfying. They now dwelled in a comfort zone, which had a whole lot more to do with convenience than desire.

But Jane's reappearance in his life—as an adult—was obviously proving to be more than Nicole could bear.

The trouble had been festering for two decades. Never apart from Greg despite their divorce, Nicole had burned each and every time he returned from a visit back home with stories of the enchanting Jane. He would relate the tales to Kevin, his best man and best friend. Nicole would first pretend not to hear, then she would listen and pretend it was jolly fun, and then she would ultimately erupt in envy. The two females had never seen each other again after the wedding, but it hadn't stopped the animosity.

He just hadn't realized until now, this minute, just how deeply agitated Nicole had grown over the years.

If Jane gave Nicole the same sort of thought, it was well concealed. She shared his father's attitude that he'd married beneath himself and had long ago corrected the oversight.

Jane didn't seem to possess an ounce of insecurity in her trim little body. And it made her all the more alluring.

So why the hell did he think more highly of her now that he'd decided not to see her anymore?

And why was he hesitating to tell Nicole that he'd broken off with her nemesis? It would make the weekend a whole lot easier.

But Greg just couldn't voice the truth, yet. It would give the breakup a bite of reality that he wasn't ready to accept.

"Okay, if you want to stick to business," Nicole snapped back. "Let's talk about my script. I can't believe you don't think it's any good!"

Greg sighed hard. "Nicole. I need a cup of coffee."

"Not until we talk!"

"You know you have a flair for a certain kind of show," he sought to explain with a rein on his temper. "Your writing on the nuclear-waste station was superb. And that how-to show you did for the schools on recycling was well received. But I don't want this series to have a hard-line approach. A search for the perfect English village should be on a more fanciful vein."

"But I took all our research, outlined every town on the route."

"I can't help but envision an approachable host, perhaps on a motorbike," he explained with a far-off look. "Exploring each town—one a week—in a lazy, easy way, drawing out the strengths of each village—"

"But they're not perfect! There're so many ills, so many troubles."

"Negatives can be put in perspective in a vague sort of way," he argued.

"Sounds like a tourist-guide job," she spat in distaste.

"Now you're getting the idea!" he rejoined, to her vehemence. "I want to do a sort of colorful travelogue. A coffeetable book of photos brought to life. Bring rural England to the thousands of Americans who will never get there."

She stomped her sandaled foot. "Silly daydream fluff!"

"By Jove, I do believe she's got it!" Kevin Cross teased, breezing in the door with a cardboard tray of coffees and a sack of doughnuts. "Morning, all."

"Why didn't you tell me Greg was going to hate my script?" she demanded, whirling on the third member of their company.

"Because I am a wimp." Kevin set his delivery on his desk and opened the sack. "Sugar or glazed, Greg?"

Greg smiled greedily at his stocky, dark-featured pal. "Caffeine!" He gingerly removed the cover from one of the insulated cups, taking a small sip of the steamy brew. "As it happens, Nicole, I wrote a script of my own. All it needs is a British humorist like Stephen Humphries to bring it alive. That's the task I want you on, Nik. Finding our host."

"All right," she glumly agreed.

"So how're Dad and the flower girl?" Kevin asked, easing into his chair.

"Both in pretty good shape right now," Greg replied, dipping a doughnut in his cup.

"Will you ever quit calling Jane Haley the flower girl?" Nicole shrilled, taking a huge bite out of a glazed pastry. "You don't call me the bride!"

"I will, if it will restore harmony around here," Kevin assured.

Nicole swallowed hard, grabbing her purse. "I hate the both of you! And this is supposed to be my day off!" With one last lethal look, she charged out the door, giving it a blind bouncing slam.

"How could I have underestimated her territorial feelings for me?" Greg questioned in bewilderment, edging his bare lean thigh onto his partner's desk.

"Ah, she's just frazzled because she can't find someone of her own," Kevin explained with a sigh. "All these years, you've both been on even ground. I think it's hard on her, seeing that gooey look on your face. It's been twenty years since she's seen it, and this time it's not for her."

"Women are nuts!" Greg curled his fingers into a fist. "I broke up with Janey, you know," he blurted out in despair.

Kevin's cheeks dimpled. "Again?"

"This time I did more than tell you," he heartily apprised. "I told *her*, too."

"That was stupid."

"Thanks."

"You'll never get her out of your system, so why fight it? At your age, it's foolish to waste the time."

"You're my age," he snapped back.

Kevin grinned, twirling a pencil. "Yeah. And probably the only ally you have at the moment. So you outta be listening to me, in a real cordial way."

Greg flashed him a pandering smile. "If it's all right with you, I'd like to get a little work done. You check into buying the rights to that private eye's autobiography? Did you interview that woman who's trying to get her son out of that jail in Iran? Any financial backers for that deep-sea expedition?" He fired their current projects at him in rapid succession.

Kevin aimed his pencil at Greg's adjoining desk. "There are all sorts of goodies in your 'In' basket. Haul your butt and your bad attitude over there for a look."

They worked in harmony for several hours. It was close to six o'clock before they began to wind down and think about drinks and dinner at their favorite Italian restaurant down the street.

The telephone bleated just as they were filing things away. Greg promptly picked it up, assuming it was one last business call.

"Grimey?" He exchanged a panicky look with Kevin. John Grimes had been Clark Baron's manservant since before Greg was born. And he rarely called the Brentwood office, unless there was real reason.

He gripped the receiver to his ear, steeling himself for the worst. "What's the matter? Has Dad taken a turn?"

"Settle down, boy. He hasn't had another attack," Grimes informed him, his voice smooth and steady. "But I do think it would be best if you returned tomorrow on an earlier flight."

Grimes had been Greg's pal his whole life. He could trust him to give him things straight. "Is he standing next you, making this demand, or is this just some friendly advice?"

There was a pause. "He's seated alone in the atrium, next to the table where I lay the mail," Grimes explained on a concerned note. "Hasn't moved an inch since he opened the letter."

"What letter?" Greg demanded in confusion.

"Well, boy... It's not for me to say."

Greg's heart began to hammer. "Maybe I should take the red-eye."

"No, actually, I imagine it will sit better for both of you after a good night's sleep. Tomorrow will do nicely. Oh, yes, Happy April Fools' Day."

He drew a surprised breath. "Is this some kind of a prank, Grimes?"

"Not by me," he replied in affront. "I'm not the one who plays around."

Greg sat immobile for a moment, the dial tone buzzing in his ear.

Kevin was hovering over his desk, full of curiosity. "So, what's up?"

Greg set the receiver back on the console. "It wasn't for him to say."

"Huh?"

"Dad got some letter," he reported, immersed in his own private confusion.

"From whom?"

"Beats me. But apparently he must need my support."

"Maybe you should call back, speak to your dad. Get a clearer picture."

Greg rubbed his square chin in speculation. "No, I trust Grimey's judgment. He knows how precious my time is on this end. Obviously this is something that Dad can't handle over the wire."

"So you still want to grab some dinner?"

Greg forced a smile. "Yeah. Sure. I'm sure it's nothing much. Grimes intimated that somebody's been playing around. But we know that Dad's way too old to be in any water hotter than tepid."

ONCE THEY WERE SETTLED in a roomy booth at the Italian eatery with plates of lasagna and glasses of red house wine in front of them, Greg opened up about all that had happened with Jane that week.

He took a long sip of burgundy as he thought back to the disappointment etched on her pretty face as he escorted her to her new post behind the notions counter in the Bargain Basement.

She'd almost succeeded in making him feel like a heel with her trembling lip, the singe of betrayal in her eyes. *Almost*.

As it was, he figured he'd done her a favor. True, commissions were minuscule down there amid the hodgepodge of low-priced merchandise. But she was out of Nibling's way. Safe from the unemployment line.

Jane didn't realize just how actively Nibling had been campaigning for her dismissal. Her personnel file was thick with his written protests, covering everything from extended lunches to the breaking of something known as a Ding-Dong Charlie doll. Greg handled the problem the best way he knew how. As if anyone ever "handled" Jane! She was all wrong for Nibling's little world. She couldn't meekly follow old ways, respect a superior without a valid reason.

He'd rehashed his decision over and over again, looking for a loophole, a better way. And now Kevin was doing the same thing.

"Look, Kev, Jane is just a small cog in a very large machine," he sought to explain with a wave of his fork.

Kevin bit into a breadstick with a shrug. "She knows that, I'm sure. Obviously she's fighting for some fresh oil and fine-tuning. Just as you are."

"Yeah, as irritating as her unpredictable behavior can be, her showy bid for sales was a step in the right direction. The Emporium needs to revamp, make an effort to reach the nineties customer.

"And it's now or never," Greg continued. "The newer stores downtown are giving the Emporium stiff competition. None of them have the prestigious reputation that we have, but their departments are streamlined for customer flow, focused shopping. Baron's was created when shopping was considered a leisurely pastime rather than a necessity. The whole operation needs hands-on attention, from the building to the personnel to the merchandise."

Images of his hands-on lady danced again in Greg's brain. He could feel a flush rising beneath his tan. Good thing the restaurant was dark.

"So it sounds like Jane had the right idea," Kevin observed in the silent lapse between them.

"Jane was right, but she was wrong!" he sought to protest with another gulp of wine. "It wasn't wise to hit Sir over the head with all of this. The old man's in total denial. This has to be handled with subtlety."

"I think he's tougher than you give him credit for," Kevin argued. "He was robust enough when I dropped in last month."

"Yeah, well, he makes people believe whatever," Greg retorted. "He even has many of the old-time employees convinced that the profits are still impressive. In any case, time is running out. The entire Emporium soon could sink like the *Titanic*. Nobody aboard would see through Sir until it was going down. The band would play on until the end."

"But it isn't too late to turn this around," Kevin coaxed, his raven brows winged in hope. "You can set everything right. If you play it smart."

GREG TREKKED BACK TO Minnesota first thing Sunday morning. With the time difference and the hours in flight, it was late in the afternoon before he arrived at his father's massive Tudor-style home. He took the long winding driveway at a good clip in his Corvette convertible, a scarlet streak on the sun-dappled green grounds. He lifted a hand to a straw-hatted figure pruning a cluster of juniper shrubs, then realized that it was Clark Baron himself.

Greg pulled to a stop in front the impressive arched entrance, eased out of the car, and started down the gently sloping lawn.

He'd already decided that Sir should set the tone, tell him when and how he pleased.

"Dad!" His greeting held an edge of confusion and humor as he surveyed his father's twill slacks and faded plaid shirt. "Thought you were the gardener in that getup. Did you let Burt go?"

"No, I didn't let Burt go," Sir retorted, turning to snap the clippers at a bush. "Just because I'm trimming a bush doesn't mean I've trimmed my staff."

Greg shoved his hands into his tan shorts, staring down at his athletic shoes to hide his dismay. Sir's fanatical blade manipulation was more a murderous chop than a trim. And his father's look proved a match for his chop. When Greg lifted his gaze again, Sir was regarding him with a homicidal gleam from beneath the brim of his hat. "I am not destitute yet, boy."

"I didn't say you were, Dad," he protested on a laugh.

"You thought it."

"I did not."

Sir snorted. "Well, you were wrong in any case. Light yard work is a prescription straight from the doctor. It's supposed to relax me."

Greg's jaw slacked in wonder. "You're kidding."

The smaller man shrugged his sloping shoulders. "Caring for growing, living things is supposed to be wonderful therapy." He gestured to a colorful flower bed closer to the house. "I planted those petunias and marigolds last week. With Burt's guidance, of course. His expertise lies in lawn care," he lectured dourly. "Always bow to someone's experience and knowledge. That way a man can learn a little bit about a lot of things."

Greg gritted his teeth behind a placid smile. The messages were coming hot and heavy. Sir was steamed. Really put out by something.

What the hell was in that letter?

Sir began clipping madly again, eating away the needled branches.

"How about you take a break from this frolic," Greg swiftly suggested. To his relief, his father actually paused in mid-snip.

"Yes, let's go out back to the patio for a drink," he suggested abruptly. "I have something to show you."

Greg allowed Sir to set the pace as they trudged up the lawn and around the side of the expansive mansion of brick and stone. As the backyard came into sight, Greg was treated to a surge of pleasant memories. It was a quiet sanctuary of oaks and elms and pines, a safe hideaway from the pressures of the world. This had been his make-believe kingdom as a child. In the winter he'd played the Alaskan tracker, the Eskimo, or blizzard-making mad scientist. On summer days like this one, he'd been anything from a forest ranger to bounty hunter to Indian chief to Tarzan.

He'd eventually played an unintentional Tarzan to a very rambunctious Jane. His gaze strayed beyond the stand of pines where he'd been dozing in a hammock during one of the Barons' annual Labor Day bashes of long ago. He'd been thirtyish and long divorced, groggily enjoying the warm autumn breeze, the gentle swing of his suspended cradle.

Her presence had seemed uncertain at first. As if it could have been the scampering of a squirrel or flutter of a bird.

But it was her, all right. He'd known it the moment her mouth covered his. Their lips had locked one long hot moment, raising the temperature and humidity of the Barons' backyard to a wet, sizzling burn.

Sixteen years old and determined to experiment.

He knew it had meant nothing real at the time. It was a case of smooch and run. It had shaken her so badly that she'd turned around an hour later and guilelessly demanded driving lessons in his Corvette in front of everybody!

He could never wander back here without thinking of that day.

There was no way to mince the facts. Sweet baby Jane was forever part of him.

Doses of her wishpower kept him shackled. Even when he knew he was all wrong for her.

Yes, moving into this old backyard was like stepping into a time warp, full of happy memories and a doting father who had always made time for him.

For that, Greg felt he owed Sir some patience and faith.

For the old times, the good times. No matter how high the times, Clark Baron had held firm to his family values. Greg and his mother, Amanda, were always well taken care of.

But nothing was ever bound to be easy or maudlin with Sir. He could be domineering, difficult and grumpy when he didn't get his way. A point he was reaffirming as he mumbled his way up to the flagstone courtyard behind the kitchen.

Grimes must have seen them coming, for he was on the spot in his summertime uniform of pale blue slacks and button-down shirt. As they seated themselves at the wrought-iron patio set, the manservant put before them a silver tray holding a pitcher of lemonade, a couple of tall glasses, and a white envelope bearing a canceled stamp and a handwritten address.

The letter. Finally!

"You know what that tray holds?" Sir demanded with a gesture.

"I'm just relieved to see that it doesn't hold your favorite ale," Greg quipped, accepting the glass Grimes was offering him.

"It holds your future!" he roared, pounding the tabletop with a tray clattering fist.

"What the hell are you talking about?" Greg queried with strained patience.

"That letter, Gregory. It's addressed to me, but it's all about you."

Greg reached for the envelope. "And who would know all about me?" He scanned the return address. "Mabel? What does she know?"

"It was sent by her, typed by her, but it isn't all about what *she* knows about you."

"Huh?"

Grimes smiled wanly. "Why don't you open it?"

Because he didn't want to. He knew all of sudden that it was all about Jane and her transfer. Sir's little princess had gone to the top with her complaint. April Fool!

"Grimes, you called me home because little Janey Haley is unhappy?" he demanded in a thin hard voice.

"Grimes called you home because I asked him to," Clark sharply corrected. "Because I wanted to confront you face-to-face!"

"Look, it just wasn't all that serious," Greg protested with a shrug of his wide shoulders. "Jane stepped out of line. It was a personnel clash—"

"Surely you mean personal," Clark corrected in affront.

"Personnel," Greg enunciated succinctly. "She went too far in the tutu."

"I don't want to know what she was wearing, when—when—" Clark huffed in disgust. "A Midwestern gentleman doesn't tell."

"Doesn't tell?" Greg drew a perplexed frown, his gaze moving from his outraged father to Grimes, hovering beside the table with quiet dignity. "Perhaps you'd just like to translate this mess to me Grimey. Get me out of this, please, like you did in the old days."

Grimes rolled his eyes skyward, heaving a sigh of defeat. "Oh, young man, I would very much enjoy that. But this is one scrape even your old Grimey can't get you out of."

Greg closed his eyes, summoning his composure. "Jane's antics—"

"Oh, is that what they call it out in California?" Sir cut in coldly.

"Well, even your old cohort Nibling called her a tease."

Sir's withered face was aghast. "Not to her face?"

"Yes, of course to her face. Haven't you spoken to him, yet?"

"He will be fired on the spot!" Sir proclaimed with the shake of a fist.

Greg shook his head in bewilderment. He knew his father was wild about Jane, but to go overboard over this demotion was beyond belief!

"Father! What's gotten into you?"

Met only by Sir's granite glare, he peeled open the envelope and unfolded the single sheet of typing paper.

He scanned the contents of the letter, his jaw dropping. "No, Dad. This just can't be!"

4

"START READING OUT LOUD," Sir directed sharply.

Greg looked up from the single-page letter in surprise to find Clark hunched over the glass-topped table like a silver wolf primed to pounce. This stress couldn't be good for his system. "Now, Dad—"

"Read!"

"Okay, okay." With a huff he began.

"Dear Sir,

I am sorry to hear that you've been under the weather. If you are still feeling unwell, please set this aside for a later look. But if you happen to be on your feet once again, I do have a problem concerning Gregory. Because you are like a father to me, and are indeed Greg's true father, I hope you won't mind intervening on my behalf.

I have found myself in a very uncomfortable condition, and your son is responsible. As you may already know, I find myself no longer on his arm."

Greg winced over the archaic phrasing.

"What's the matter with that?" Sir defensively demanded.

Greg cleared his throat, making an effort to control his twitching mouth. Jane might be the mastermind here, but Mabel was certainly responsible for wording aimed for Sir's empathy. "Nothing. Nothing at all." He continued on. "'And it seems to me to be no coincidence that, directly after our breakup, I find myself banished to the Bargain Basement.'"

"Unthinkable," Sir scoffed. "A Haley in the basement!"

"It was a necessary move," Greg sought to explain. "A temporary stopover until I can figure what to do with her." Sir's face darkened. "Keeping reading."

"Please know that I did first appeal to Gregory. But instead of showing me the sort of understanding our long-term relationship deserves, he took the coward's way out, shuffling me out of the way! I suspect that he hoped the demotion would pressure me into quitting altogether. That, of course, would be the ultimate answer to avoiding any future discomfort, quelling any in-store gossip concerning us as a couple."

Greg took a steadying breath, eyeing his father again. "It's true that I hope the employees won't get the details of my affair with Jane, but it isn't the reason I transferred her to the basement."

"It gets better," Sir prompted brusquely, motioning to the paper.

"As it is, the basement won't be deep or dim enough to conceal my newfound condition for long. Exhaustion and teariness can perhaps be somehow explained away with some small excuse. But the swelling is another matter entirely. If you haven't already guessed, Sir, I am pregnant. And Gregory is responsible."

Greg broke off, his jaw sagging loose. He swiftly read on.

"My head is spinning right now. Because of my delicate state, but also over my uncertain future as a mother.

I know how proud you are of Gregory. He's always been a hero of mine, too, coming through whenever I've needed assistance. But lately he's shown an egotistical bullheaded streak, which has shaken my faith. I am frightened that he has me trapped this way. Don't let him ruin me!"

Clark pounded the table. "This is disgraceful!"

To Greg it was unbelievable. He'd grown entirely numb, aside from the blood thrumming in his ears. He read on under Clark's laser gaze.

"Any chances I've taken, any moves I've made, have been with the best intentions. I expected to be rewarded, not shunned, for my efforts. Is it too much to expect some compensation?"

"I'd give up the whole Emporium for a grandchild!" Sir interrupted on a bellow.

"A fact I'm sure she knows," Greg retorted tightly.

"I hope you will understand that I find my present circumstances unbearable. Since Gregory seems unusually preoccupied with rings, perhaps it's about time he take the one out of your nose, Sir, mount it with a respectable-size diamond, and slip it on a finger where it will really do him some good!

Lovingly yours, Janey.

P.S. I don't think you'd make a grouchy gramps at all."

Greg held the letter in trembling fingers. When he'd referred to Sir as a grouchy gramps in the office on Friday, he hadn't meant it in a literal sense! But she'd obviously filed it away for later use. She must have known by then that she was pregnant. Must have been holding back the fact to use as a trump card if he didn't take her back of his own free will. How dare she demand a ring from him through his father? He scanned the letter again, studying the message. She'd actually requested compensation before she'd suggested marriage! The whole thing seemed so calculated, so opportunistic. Why hadn't she told him first? Given him the chance to make it right?

Because she wanted results. Swift, sure action.

Greg fought the desire to crumple the paper in his hand. Sir was grinning in grim triumph. He didn't like untraditional relationships. But he did finally have his son caught in the fatherhood noose!

"If she terminates that pregnancy because of your egotistical bullheadedness—"

"I'm not those things! I don't care what she claims!"

A vein throbbed at Sir's temple. "If she does, I'll…I'll…"

Have another heart attack without delay, Greg thought frantically. "Settle down, Dad, please."

"How could I have raised such a scoundrel of a son?"

"You didn't. You know it. Just as I *didn't* know about the baby."

"What's that remark about me being a grouchy gramps mean, then?"

"Oh, it was taken out of context," Greg muttered in dismissal. "I swear that she mentioned nothing about any baby to me."

"Swear on your mother's memory?"

So it had sunk that low. "Yes," he answered promptly. "I shouldn't have to, but I will."

Clark slumped back in his brightly cushioned chair with an audible sigh of relief.

"Dad, I transferred Jane because Nibling demanded her resignation," he explained. "Jane put on a circus to promote play-yard equipment and Nibling blew his stack. It was a way to satisfy everyone. I know how much you respect Nibling and I understand your paternal feelings for Jane. They needed to be separated fast. I put Jane in the only open spot in the whole damn store!"

Clark brushed aside the shoptalk with a sweep of his hand. "So Jane will be the one to give me my grandchild, after all. We'll make it as easy as possible for her, make sure she has the best of everything. She needn't worry about working in the store at all anymore. All she has to do is take good care of herself, and be the wonderful mother I know she can be." He leveled a finger at his son with a stern look. "You just have to make certain that she does intend to go through with this. That she doesn't grow too despondent and do something foolish."

"Jane obviously doesn't want to terminate this pregnancy," Greg hastened to soothe. "She could have done so without a word. Instead she's reaching out to you for help because she loves and trusts you."

"Well, she loves no one on earth more thoroughly than you, Greg," he raved with disgust. "You've been a blind fool not to acknowledge the fact long ago. But the time has come to set right your fate. It's up to you to get over to her place and propose on bended knee."

Greg bared his teeth. What he felt like doing was turning her over his knee for a paddling. How dare she try and trap him into marriage!

Clark gave a sudden, wistful smile. "You know, I truly believe it's what she's always wanted, since the day of your first wedding."

"Really think so?" Greg demanded sarcastically.

"Go to her, son, with ring in hand. Here," he said dryly with an extended palm. "Take this metaphoric one from my nose along. Lead her around with it for a change. If you can."

"Very amusing, Dad." He would get her for this sneaky maneuver. And he would have things his way from here on in. Miss Jane Haley was going to get exactly what she'd been fishing for, for the past two decades!

JANE ARRIVED AT WORK Monday morning at the usual time of eight-thirty, dressed in a somber gray suit and pink blouse, her raven mane pulled back in a barrette. She shuffled into the elevator car, sluggishly directing the operator down to the basement rather than up to the second-floor toy department. She couldn't help dwelling on last Friday's excitement, when she'd taken this same ride with her yellow costume in her white tote.

She'd soared high then, been smug about putting everything into her job. It was too bad she always gave her heart so freely. It was taking this new drop with her. As was her stomach, she suddenly realized, groping for the wall bar to steady herself. She certainly wasn't handling this setback with her usual verve. And it was so important to keep up a sassy front for the Barons. She hadn't heard from father or son all weekend.

Something was bound to happen this morning. Unless Mabel put the wrong address on the letter, or Sir just wasn't up to reading it. If Clark Baron hadn't gotten her message, she would be trapped in that underground jungle of odors indefinitely.

She'd had to bite her tongue with every transaction last Friday afternoon. A young waiter from one of the downtown restaurants had dashed in for a new tie to replace the soiled one around his neck. He was low on cash so had ultimately been shooed down to the basement. The gaudy print that had fit his budget had been simply awful. Then there was the secretary who had promised her boss she'd pick up some toiletries for the executive rest room. She'd walked away with a novelty kit left over from Christmas, with soap and cologne and shaving cream—all in pine-scented green.

Considering herself a humanitarian, making those sales had seemed almost criminal!

The lady responsible for stocking the merchandise was waiting for Jane when the elevator doors opened. Audrey Pallack stood behind the central counter with a cheery wave of a jelly doughnut. Brassy, lazy Audrey. With her hair too red, her dresses too tight, and her manners too earthy. An old-time employee who'd managed the basement for centuries, who'd risen to a senior level by sheer staying power. She'd trained scores of rookie clerks over the years, sending them up to bigger things once they got the Emporium sales format down pat. Audrey proclaimed herself an indispensable mentor, whose tutorship kept the store on an even foundation. But everyone knew—aside from Sir, it seemed—that she loved the basement because she could hide away her days in the stockroom, watching daytime TV and munching on junk food. She let the youngsters do the work while she lounged around.

Jane didn't approve, but was grateful for the slack, after Nibling's intense nit-picking. In any case, she hoped the whole setback would be only temporary.

"Mornin', Jane!"

Jane gulped with a forced smile as Audrey took a huge bite of her jelly doughnut. She chewed vigorously, obviously struggling to swallow. "Don't even bother to set your purse down, hon. Little Sir wants to see you upstairs."

Jane's brows lifted in hope. "Oh yeah?"

"Yeah. In Infants."

"You have any more details?"

Audrey pulled a finger around her sugar-encrusted lips. "Nope. Which means no details have leaked." She heaved her sizable bosom. "Gee, I'd hate to lose ya, though. Hell, maybe I won't."

Hell, maybe you will. Jane nodded and marched back into an open elevator.

Jane glanced at her watch as the operator bulleted them directly up to the fifth floor. The store wasn't set to open for another fifteen minutes. There was just enough time for a reassignment. She could be in place greeting customers without a misstep. Which was something Greg didn't seem to appreciate about her. She was damn good at her job. Adaptable to any corner of the store. Maybe he had come to realize it, she thought with a glimmer of satisfaction. Or maybe Sir had laid down an order. In any case, she would be free of the basement.

Greg was waiting in the center of the department. Dressed in a gray suit similar in shade to her own, he was easy enough to spot in the pastel jumble of baby clothing and accessories. He was standing near a double-decker rack of tiny sunsuits, his body language revealing his discomfort. His arms were folded across the breadth of his chest and his lean hip was cocked at a sharp angle.

Maybe he was on guard because he was about to own up to making a mistake. A first in their long relationship.

"Good morning, Greg," she said brightly.

He turned on his heel, towering over her with a dangerous glitter in his eyes. "It's mister in the store," he returned curtly.

"Nobody's within twenty yards of us," she protested, gesturing to the two clerks busily setting up a stroller display.

"Wisely so. They can sense a storm warning when they see one, Miss Haley."

"All right, Mr. Baron," she said with a toss of her head. Obviously this was all business to him. She was grateful, now, that she had worn her best power suit. She'd been far easier to rattle in her tutu. "So what do you want?"

Greg slipped a hand into his suit jacket and removed her letter from the lining pocket.

"So Sir did get it!"

"He got it, all right."

Jane blinked. "I hope you're not too angry about this whole thing. I mean, my future is at stake."

"Oh, yes, I believe that was mentioned in here somewhere." He opened the letter and scanned it.

"So, is there an opening for me up here in Infants?" she prompted.

He was nonplussed by her nerve. "No, of course not!"

She gasped at his terse tone. "Then what is going on? Why are we here?"

"Because it seemed like the perfect place to hammer out your deal, decide on just what form of compensation you're demanding."

Jane shook her head in bewilderment. "I only wanted my share of the commissions made down in Toys on Friday."

He cocked a sardonic brow. "Is that all? You sure?"

"Well, I really deserve a share of all the Plas-Tek sales made in the upcoming week. But perhaps that's too big a dream—" She halted in midsentence, realizing that he was mocking her. "Greg, it isn't like you to play games."

"You started this game and I'm just playing along." Taking hold of her arm, he steered her even farther away from the clerks, into an out-of-the-way aisle shelving bibs and diapers. "Now, Father and I both want you to pick out whatever it is you need to get your nest feathered."

"This is nuts!" She wrenched free of his grasp. "I never thought I'd hear myself saying this, but I'm going back to the basement."

"No, you aren't." He caught her shoulder in his huge hand, digging his fingers into the padding of her jacket.

Jane's heart began to hammer as she looked up into his eyes, silvered with raw fury. "What's the matter with you?" he hissed under her breath.

"I can't believe that this is the real you, Jane. Conniving, greedy, sneaky."

"I just want a respectable place with Baron's," she retorted in a hush.

"You've shot for the top, all right," he congratulated bitterly. "You took your complaint and your condition to the top man and he's ready to lay it all down for you. Make your life leisurely and secure."

Her small features softened. "Well, you don't look too happy about your decision."

"I'm talking about *Sir*, you fool!"

Jane paused, a protest lodging in her throat. She swallowed it back down because she did indeed feel the fool. It was a foreign, seldom-felt state. Greg had to be the only man on earth who could still reduce her to an awkward, bungling child. But why would he want to do that?

"Greg," she began in a stumble. "I can't believe you're this angry over such a small issue—"

"*Small?* Your condition is small stuff?"

"Well, once I realized just what my condition was, I tried to reach you at break time. But you'd already left for California."

"Let me get this straight," he said in quiet confusion. "You went down to the basement after lunch. Realized by two-thirty that you are pregnant—"

"That I'm what?"

He wasn't even connecting with her dismay, so sure of his facts with the letter to back him up. "You use some sort of home test from the pharmacy?"

"Well, I did go down to the pharmacy from your office—"

"Ah, now we're cutting to the chase."

"I went to the pharmacy for—"

"I know, for verification." He rolled his eyes with a moan. "I take the blame for the protection." His voice dropped to the barest whisper. "That first time, on Valentine's Day..."

"Will you let me get a word in?" she pressed.

"Look, just take what you need," he broke in angrily, grabbing a box of cloth diapers, shoving them into her arms. "You went to Sir for help and he's rarin' to give it to you."

She took a step back. "I don't want those!"

"Well, we don't sell disposables."

She opened her mouth in another attempt to deny the pregnancy, explain that she'd purchased tissues for her runny nose, but decided to first take stock of exactly what he was saying, and where he stood. He had apparently misunderstood the content of the letter, believing that her allergic symptoms were caused by pregnancy. The mistake would have been uproarious, if he weren't so angry about the prospect. Breaking up had been tough enough. But to have this sort of rejection slapped so plainly in one's face, to lose all hope of a future, was so devastating and humiliating. Greg knew full well that had been her dream since childhood.

She took a steadying breath, tipping her face up to meet his burning glare. "So let me get this straight. You don't want any child of mine, is that it?"

"I don't like your underhanded methods," he hedged, "using my father to bring me 'round."

Jane nodded thoughtfully, aware that customers would be trickling in any minute. "Okay, I'll take you up on this compensation deal. You can give me what I need."

"Dad invites you to run a tab."

"Oh, I don't think that will be necessary."

"Perhaps not today—"

"Not any day soon." Jane took the diapers from him, turning the package over in her hands. "First of all, these are way too large for the dribbles I'm expecting."

"How many sizes are there?" He watched with open perplexity as she stepped past him and set them back on the shelf.

"Don't look so damn frightened," she consoled with a sweet smile. "I'm actually going to be a bargain. Imagine, a bargain from the Bargain Basement. How fitting."

"But I told you, Jane, you won't be working down there or anyplace else in the store from here on in."

"Oh, just incubating the baby for your father is to be job enough, is that it?"

"Apparently, yes. If that's what you want. Just tell me what you need now. Today. It's yours."

"Well, one of these should get me through the worst of it." With a necromancer's flourish she whisked the hankie out of his top pocket and gave her nose a mighty blow.

"Hey! Janey!"

"This is all I need, you big oaf," she fumed in open anger. "I didn't think it was possible, but you and Sir have managed to take all the magic out of having a Baron baby."

He whitened. "Janey, please. You can't even consider terminating your—"

"If I could terminate my condition, I would!" She grinned into his mortified face. "The teariness, the dizziness, the swelling I mentioned in the letter were all part of an allergic reaction to the stock downstairs."

"You mean you're not having a baby?" he asked in sheer disbelief.

Jane's eyes glittered blue chips. "By Jove, I think he's got it!"

"But the letter..."

"You and Sir misunderstood, that's all," she snapped. "Forget about the letter and forget about me. I'm giving up on you Barons. I'll willingly spend the duration of my time here down in the Bargain Basement. The lack of customers will give me plenty of time to draft a new résumé. Good day, Mr. Baron."

"But there has to be a baby," he sputtered in confusion.

"Thank goodness there isn't, considering the welcome the poor mite was getting." With that parting remark, Jane stuffed his used hankie back in his pocket and marched off.

JANE WASN'T BACK IN THE basement for fifteen minutes when she regretted giving Greg back his hankie. She was in the middle of ringing up a ninety-nine-cent pair of heart-figured anklets for a young career woman when she had a sneezing fit.

She accepted the box of tissues from a disgruntled Audrey, who'd torn herself away from the television to rescue her.

"I'm so sorry," Jane told the disapproving customer with a dab to her nose. "But it's my allergies."

The young blonde in the pretty red dress accepted her sack and penny change with a sympathetic look. "Actually, I was lost in my own thoughts. These socks weren't exactly what I was looking for. I just hate to make do, but I guess sometimes there's no other option here, downtown."

Once the woman had departed, Jane turned to Audrey with a sniffle. "I keep hearing that remark over and over again."

"Oh, hell, don't we all just make do?" Audrey complained hurriedly, reaching under the counter for a candy bar. "Got to get back to 'People's Court,' hon. It's a doozy of a duel over a dog bite."

Jane watched her superior lumber back between the stockroom curtains. "No, Audrey, we don't all just make do," she muttered aloud. In spite of the fact that she would be leaving the Baron fold soon, she couldn't help envisioning a totally modernized basement, with better service and merchandise. If only she could find a way to tolerate the scents! She could make this floor the real foundation of the store.

She fought an internal battle the rest of the day, her resentment for Greg and Sir in conflict with her creative visions. In the end, both had gotten an equal share of her time. She left the store with a mental résumé and a whole new approach to Bargain Basement selling.

5

JANE RECOGNIZED THE rumble of Greg's Corvette as she unlocked her black Saturn sedan. The three-level parking garage adjacent to the store was almost empty of customers and clerks alike, by now. She'd lagged behind after closing to take a cursory inventory of the basement's stock, so she could spend the night formulating some new sales angles. Of course she'd hoped to avoid just this sort of confrontation, as well. Greg was known to be out the office door with the last of the customers. But he'd obviously been staking out here in the employee section of the garage, waiting for her to appear.

Once her anger had ebbed to a simmer, she'd begun to wonder just what Mabel had put in that letter. Surely she couldn't have gone off the deep end with a pregnancy claim! Mabel would never toy that way with Sir.

In any case, it really didn't matter. Greg was mortified over the thought. Had broken up with her for good.

So why was Mr. Big Shot bumper to bumper with her? Revving his motor with an anxious foot?

"Jane," he called out over the engine's purr. "Get in the car."

She half turned toward the convertible to meet his demand with a glare. "I'm trying to."

"*My car!*"

He might as well have invited her into the fires of hell! "No, thanks."

"C'mon, something's screwy here."

"You must mean someone," she corrected tersely. "But, hey, no sense in being so hard on yourself. Nutty rich people are considered delightfully eccentric by the rest of the more humble population."

Greg gripped the steering wheel with white knuckles. In all the years he'd known Jane, she'd never once thrown the Baron wealth at him. No matter how angry she'd been. But perhaps this pregnancy thing was affecting her emotions. Was she or wasn't she? He had to know the truth!

"Jane," he began on a silky note. "This is no place to hash this thing out."

"I think we've slung enough hash to last us a lifetime," she cried, flailing her arms. "You should be doing eighty down the highway by now, whooping for joy that I've given up on you."

"Why did you send such a crazy letter to Dad?" he demanded, his temper straining. "Don't you know how fragile he is right now?"

She walked over to the open car door, resting her hand on the edge of the windshield. "I didn't expect to upset him at all. I figured he'd shake his head over your ignorance, make a few calls to the store, and get me out of the basement. Simple."

Except for the pregnancy! She was glossing right over that again. Greg gritted his teeth. Why would she be in denial now? He couldn't bear the suspense. And neither could Sir. The proud grandpapa-to-be expected to see both of them at the estate tonight. Greg couldn't even get her into his car and he felt like a bumbling fool for it.

"Look, Janey, I'm assuming Mabel typed the letter. You're from the school of hunt and peck, and the phrasing is prehistoric."

"I dictated. She typed. So what?"

"Did you proofread it?"

"What's the difference?" she lamented. "You don't want me anymore, anyway."

"Will you get off that single-minded track for just a minute?"

"Your charm is overwhelming! How do you keep those California beauties off you?"

"You're so wound up in your feelings that you can't give me a straight answer on anything," he complained. Without warning he lunged across the seat. He clamped one hand on her arm and opened the passenger door with the other.

"Let me go!"

"We are going to read this letter together, here and now."

Keeping his body nudged against hers, he reached over to shut off the engine.

Jane sighed hard, taking the familiar paper in hand. "All right! I can't believe how you managed to read so much between the lines. I—" She broke off as she absorbed Mabel's polished version of the message. She had actually done it. *Announced that Jane was with child!*

"Between the lines, eh?"

"Oops." Jane blushed and cringed, meeting his gaze with reluctance. She would have liked to slap the sardonic smile from his face, but she was so in the wrong she didn't dare.

"So, can you explain this?" he demanded in exasperation.

Jane crumpled a little on the soft white seat. "I clearly dictated my complaints about the loss of commission and my allergic reactions to the stock. She had it all down. I looked."

Greg was a bundle of emotions. He was not to be a father, after all. He felt a niggle of loss. But it was swiftly overwhelmed with a warm glow of relief. Raising a child was such a profound responsibility. A confining commitment.

Jane made a noise of disgust as she again scanned the paper. "If you believed the letter, you believed I was looking for compensation for my pregnancy! That I was trying to force your father into a corner!"

"Dad didn't mind," he hedged.

"Oh, Greg!"

"I had hoped you wouldn't come to that realization," he confessed. "But put yourself in my place. I was shocked and upset. Figured a squeeze play was beneath you."

"Ha! It's a squeeze play that left the possibility open in the first place!"

"Allowing Mabel to type the message was the mistake," he swiftly countered. "How did it get by you?"

"I fell asleep during the rewrite stage."

"Oh, Janey! You know Mabel's work has always needed a last look."

"She mailed it before I had the chance. It seemed so simple a job."

"You would've realized there was a glaring error this morning if you hadn't been so personally affronted—"

"Of course I was affronted," she retorted defensively. "It was the final insult between us. You not wanting a baby of ours."

"I've tried my best not to lead you on. I've always been honest."

Jane tossed the letter at him and stared out the windshield. "Now that you know the truth, I hope you'll just leave me alone."

He fingered the raven tendrils that had escaped her barrette. "You deserve better than a veteran wanderer like me. And we will fix this job situation somehow. You can't quit Baron's, not when you really don't want to. From your end, I expect your help with Dad. He weathered the news of the pregnancy far better than he's going to take this false alarm.

He's expecting us at his place tonight. To discuss wedding plans."

Jane bit her lip, blinking away the moisture in her eyes. So close to her dream, yet so far. They could have been so good together, if only Greg had come to his senses, taken a chance on family life.

"I'll meet you over at the estate later on tonight," she offered tightly. "I'll corral Mabel and we'll all tackle Sir together."

Greg nodded, his face sheeted in relief. "Okay." He leaned over and kissed her cheek. "Friends?"

"Rot in hell." She popped out of the vintage convertible, giving the door an extra-hard slam.

"Hey, don't do that!" he hollered in horror.

"This crummy car is the only kind of baby you could ever appreciate, you jerk!"

"I thought we were okay with this!"

"I'm helping out for Sir's sake alone! But you are right about one thing. I do deserve better than you!"

Jane turned away as he peeled down the concrete ramp, frustrated that the tears springing to her eyes had nothing to do with her allergies.

JANE WAS IN STRONGER spirits by the time she greeted a formally dressed Grimes at the front door of Clark Baron's home later that evening. She'd changed into comfortable wheat-colored slacks and a lightweight pink sweater. Sir had always liked her in pink. Said it was the "cotton-candy topping on his favorite doll."

She stepped into the huge foyer, taking perusal of the glittering crystal chandelier hanging two-and-a-half stories straight above her, the gleaming tiled floor at her feet, and the glossed walnut staircase winding upward to the private quarters. There was nothing new, really, but everything seemed so ... polished.

"I'm to take you directly to the living room," Grimes announced. She drew a wry smile as she fell into step behind him, their heels echoing in the quietness. Perhaps Greg had already broken the news to his father and they were stewing together. Poor Sir. She'd have liked nothing better than to make his dreams come true. Could he handle watching them die, without dying a little himself?

Grimes halted in his tracks in the middle of the foyer as the sliding paneled doors leading to the living room opened and Greg emerged, tight-lipped and ashen. To her surprise, he was still dressed in the suit he'd worn to work that day.

"Hi," she ventured. "I know I promised to bring Mabel, but I can't seem to track her down."

"Look no further, Jane," Grimes interceded warmly. "Mrs. Haley has been here for quite some time."

"Thank you, Grimes," Greg uttered. "I will take over."

"That would be a most welcome development, Gregory." With a small nod and twinkling eyes, he strode off down a hallway leading to the pantry.

"I've been calling all over town for my grandmother," Jane confided in frustration. "It never occurred to me that she was here."

Greg clasped her shoulders. "I tried to warn you, but your line was busy, then your machine kicked in...."

"Well, has Mabel explained herself, gotten us out of this jam? She is the logical person to right this wrong."

"Well, she hasn't made a move to do so," Greg declared grimly.

"I don't understand it! She knows Sir's always been quick to forgive her slipups. How can she look him in the eye and not straighten him out?"

"Mabel's been here long enough to really get caught up in this misconception. Dad can be as persuasive as a steamroller," he reminded her. "Now that he is fragile physically, it only heightens his dominative powers."

"Understood, but—"

The doors slid open a crack again and Clark Baron himself emerged. "Ah, Jane! We were just talking about you! Come along—"

"In a minute, Dad," Greg promised, with a halting gesture.

"Nonsense!" Sir beckoned to Jane, opening the doors wider. "Come."

Jane eased by Greg's large, stiff form. "Would another minute really matter?"

"You be the judge," Greg murmured in her ear, turning on his heel to follow her. Jane stepped into the huge opulent living room of green and gold, instantly freezing on the huge Oriental rug under her Nikes. The room was alive with people! And decorated like a mini wedding chapel!

The regal living area full of splendorous Chippendale and Duncan Phyfe had been transformed into something off the Vegas strip. A wooden arch fronted a pentagon-shaped dais. A runner extended from the arch, dividing the three rows of slatted folding chairs. Everything was white, aside from the flowers. Hundreds of roses in a rainbow of colors were set throughout the room.

"By the way," Greg added, "that is a real judge over by the china cabinet. The stout man in the brown suit, speaking to the mayor."

"Attention, everyone!" Sir announced. "The bride has arrived!"

Bride? Yes, and witnesses . . . Jane absorbed the scene and its meaning in numb slow motion. *Her own wedding was in progress.* Details like the guest list had been chosen for her.

As had the gift preferences, she realized, noting the silver-and-white packages on display atop the antique supper table.

Boy, oh boy, did she need a new can opener. But she was relatively certain that the treasures beneath the wrappings were pricey and useless. In all fairness, it would be tough to choose a gift for someone who owned his own department store.

She released a nervous giggle over their quandary and her own. She wasn't getting married to Greg and she'd be buying her own damn can opener!

Clark Baron moved to the center of the room, clapped his hands together and a discreet round of applause rippled through the air. Jane pulled a tight smile across her paling, porcelain face, her bright blue eyes frantically searching for Mabel, the one and only person she expected to find in here. Ironically, her grandmother was nowhere in sight.

Grimes entered moments later with a uniformed maid. Both were carrying trays of champagne glasses. Grimes lowered his tray in front of Jane. "Yours is the off-color one. Ginger ale." Jane met his eyes briefly as she took the crystal flute with the darker liquid. And he winked at her! Staid old Grimes had a sly side?

Of course, he, too, thought she was pregnant! A natural presumption, considering that nothing ever happened around here without his knowledge. But this time, nothing had happened!

Clark came up beside her and gave her shoulders a fatherly squeeze, much like the one he'd given her at her high school graduation.

"Nice work, m'dear," he congratulated. The very words he'd uttered that day.

Jane's mouth sagged in regret. This time she was going to be letting him down. Thinking back, she realized she'd never before had to disappoint him. "Oh, Sir, you shouldn't have done this without consulting me first. I mean, you really shouldn't have."

"Perhaps it was a little high-handed," he whispered back. "But I love you so. And shall love the daylights out of that baby, too."

"I must speak to you about the baby," Jane insisted softly. "Right, Greg?"

"Yes, Dad—"

"Oh, you shut up," Sir muttered. "You've acted the lad for twenty-five years, now you will act the doting husband for the next forty!" His features immediately softened as he returned his full attention to Jane. "Surely you see my reasoning for all of this. No one need know about your condition, as we're taking swift action. The dates will be close enough to cloud the issues, keep the tongues still."

"But to invite all of these prominent people," Greg objected, his steely eyes scoping the guests.

"They're just the gang from our annual Labor Day backyard barbecue," Sir stated matter-of-factly. "We've all been friends for years, and we made promises to include one another in these milestones. It's costing me, but by God, I've gotten efficient results!"

Jane hadn't even considered the bills. But it would all add up—the liquor, catering, flowers. Naturally it wouldn't be near the cost of a long drawn-out affair, but it would be a dead loss when they didn't do their part!

"Look here, son," Sir continued on a confidential note. "I went along with your first fiasco when it was damn obvious that you were making a poor match. You can't blame me for shunning the idea of a city-hall wedding when you've finally chosen an angel."

Jane noted that people were beginning to move closer to their trio. It seemed as though their conversation had taken an eternity, when in fact only a few minutes had passed. "Sir, where is my grandma? I'd like to speak to her."

"Upstairs in Gregory's old bedroom with the seamstress," Sir replied with a pat to her arm. "Go on ahead. It's about time you got ready, anyway."

Jane's heart hammered in her chest, raring to attack this misunderstanding from its original source. "Pardon me."

Jane glided through the sliding doors, then once out of sight she scurried across the foyer and up the huge staircase, taking a left on the top landing and another left at the second doorway. She charged inside the bedroom, nearly colliding with a headless dressmaker's model displaying a dazzling wedding dress of chiffon and taffeta. Mabel was on her knees with a small ruler, measuring the hem of the stiff ruffled skirt.

"Finally, a human dummy!" Mabel rejoiced, seeing her granddaughter.

"You should talk!" Jane cried, with a hand cocked on her hip.

"Oh, you know what I mean," Mabel chirped.

Jane's eyes widened as she took in the details of the garment. "Why, that looks like my flower-girl dress!"

"As close as I could come," Mabel declared proudly. Jane stepped up to help the old lady to her feet. "I took it out of mothballs and brought it along to the store. Clever, eh?"

Jane felt a rush of irritation and dismay. This wasn't the sort of dress she would have chosen! She didn't wish to look like an overgrown flower girl in Greg's eyes, press him into remembering what she'd done during his first ceremony. What was she saying? There weren't going to be any vows. Greg didn't wish to marry her. She had to make Mabel see that.

Jane slid her stormy gaze to the young blond seamstress, who had straightened and was fingering the measuring tape slung around her neck. "Would you give us a moment alone?"

"The dress is ready, anyway," the woman murmured, moving for the heavy mahogany door. "Congratulations."

Keeping in mind that the seamstress was an innocent bystander, Jane managed a lukewarm smile. "Yes, thank you."

Mabel's lavender taffeta gown rustled as she came rushing up the instant they were alone, clasping Jane's hands in her plump wrinkled ones. "Finally, the dream's coming true! The Haleys and the Barons, linked through marriage!" When Jane's distressed expression didn't waver, Mabel gave her hands a shake. "You are getting Greg's undivided attention. Finally!"

Jane again inspected the enlarged version of her flower-girl dress, here in Greg's old quarters. Greg was long gone by the time she was old enough to utilize this youthful, masculine room full of books, cars and model airplanes. She'd spent many solitary hours up here as a child, enjoying Greg's possessions, assuming her role as a part of the Baron clan.

"Grandma, I understand what you're trying to do for me. But this wasn't the way to bring Greg around."

"I'm just hastening the process," she stated guilelessly. "Time's running short. At the rate you were moving along, he was bound to end up back in California, still single."

Jane clamped her hands to her cheeks. "You really don't understand how all of this got started, do you?"

"I think I do. I *know* I do," she affirmed with a sound nod of her head of curls.

"This situation grew from your mishandling of the letter."

Mabel pursed her lips smugly. "I mailed it. Sir received it. It's really the simplest part of this whole thing. Just like rolling around on a log."

"It's the contents, Grandma," Jane ventured to explain. "You must have realized that right away, when Sir contacted you. You should've put the brakes on this extravaganza before it got out of control!"

There was a single knock on the door and Greg entered. "Good evening, Mabel," he said evenly. "Have we made any headway on this end?"

"Oh, yes," Mabel gushed, gesturing to the dress. "Isn't it breathtaking?"

"I do seem to recall the style," he retorted, stroking his rigid jaw.

Jane slanted him a doleful look. "Greg, do you have the letter on you?"

"Oh, yes." He extracted it from the inner pocket of his suit jacket and handed it to Mabel.

"Where're my reading glasses?" Mabel wondered aloud..

"Around your neck on a chain." Greg patiently took the frames in his fingers and set them gingerly atop Mabel's nose.

"Ah, much better," she said, unfolding the paper.

Jane clasped her hands together, sidling up to the other woman. "Now, Grandma, don't you agree that this letter is a little different from the one I dictated to you?"

Mabel's lashes fluttered. "Oh! Oh, my, yes. It is a bit tangled up in itself."

"Please back me up here and tell Greg that it was only my job I was after," Jane beseeched.

Mabel regarded him over the tops of her lenses. "That is true, Gregory."

Greg balked at her, his temper straining at the seams. "But you went so far! This letter doesn't read as a jumble at all. It seems amazingly concise in its own goofy way. And now my father is waiting down there for a wedding and a grandchild!"

Mabel's bosom heaved with impatience as she peeled off her glasses. "Now, Gregory, do you love my granddaughter or not?"

"That has nothing—"

"I am asking you a simple question!"

"Nothing is ever simple with a Haley, but yes, ma'am, I certainly do. In my own way."

"And we all know Janey returns those feelings," she lilted back dreamily. "Most of the time," she added over Jane's gasp of dismay. "So just get married and stop making this ridiculous fuss over one little letter!"

"This isn't the way I imagined it!" Jane cried out.

"Just accept his proposal," Mabel urged, again focused on the dress.

Greg was flabbergasted by their nerve. "If you ladies don't mind, I don't recall proposing anything! Don't you think I deserve the chance?"

"Of course," Mabel poohed-poohed. "You play a very important role. Very. This lace is still a little loose around the bosom," she fretted. "Where is the needle and thread?"

"I can't believe you and Dad did all this!" he exploded.

Mabel picked up a pincushion from Greg's old writing desk. "Just trying to fix your life."

"But it isn't broken," he retorted. "I don't appreciate this interference."

"Well, don't blow a gasket," Jane huffed, with her hands on her hips. "I didn't say yes, either."

"But she means yes," Mabel insisted.

Greg aimed his last-ditch appeal at Jane. "I'd like to tell Dad the truth, but I'm afraid the upset might trigger another attack. And the embarrassment this fiasco is bound to cause is something he'd never be able to recover from." He grimaced. "It's like he's holding an invisible shotgun in his hands."

Jane rubbed her temples. "I don't think our relationship can sink lower than this moment."

"Will you marry me, Jane?" Greg asked abruptly.

"That wasn't a dare!" she squealed in indignation. "I wasn't challenging you to sink lower!"

"But I thought it's what you wanted!" he thundered.

"Only if it's of your own free will, fool!"

"Let me speak to her alone, Gregory," Mabel commanded, with a shooing hand. "Besides, you aren't supposed to see the bride in her dress before the ceremony. It's bad luck."

"It wouldn't have to be forever, of course," he reasoned on his way out. "It's not like you're really pregnant."

Jane clenched her fists, narrowing her eyes to slits. "Get out of here!"

"Do it for Dad," he beseeched as Mabel closed the door.

"That rotten man!"

Mabel clucked in disapproval. "Now, Janey, he's the one you've always wanted."

Jane sighed hard. "You don't seem to give a whit that you started this. That it was your mention of a baby in that letter that ignited this whole mess!"

Mabel shrugged. "I admit that I botched up the message a little."

"Yes . . ." Jane prompted tartly.

"It should've been two separate letters, for certain," Mabel went on apologetically. "One concerning your demotion and allergies, and another announcing your pregnancy."

Jane's features crumpled. "Huh?"

Mabel looked at her with dancing eyes. "Don't tell me, dear, that you still don't understand, that you are indeed carrying a child?"

6

GREG WASN'T DOWNSTAIRS fifteen minutes when Sir's upstairs maid came in to announce that the ceremony would be proceeding on schedule. He made an attempt to charge back up the stairs to find out what was behind Jane's change of heart, but Sir and his cronies kept him boxed in, with all the old clichéd tales about marital bliss. Then Grimes took him firmly by the arm to his bedroom behind the kitchen to assist Greg into a brand-new tuxedo.

Greg couldn't believe Jane had given in without more of a guarantee from him. Without some crawling, some begging, some assurances that he wanted her with his whole heart. But she appeared on cue at the first chord of the organ music, descending the huge sweeping mahogany staircase, her petite figure full of poise.

He couldn't help remembering the last time he'd seen her in white chiffon. Her demeanor was very much the same these twenty years later, with her petulant chin and snapping eyes. She'd held true to her nature, was still every bit as bold, demanding and impetuous. Accustomed to getting exactly what she wanted. But her wishes at the moment were distorted in his mind. She'd made it clear that the terms of this union didn't appeal to her at all.

So why the change of heart?

She simply had to be doing it for Sir.

Greg was damn lucky and he knew it. He'd make it worth her while somehow.

Jane kept a steady smile as she floated down the stairs in the filmy layered dress, a bouquet of pale yellow roses in her trembling hands. The guests were crowded into the foyer, Greg standing in the forefront beside the massive carved newel post.

The trepidation marring his handsome face made her stomach lurch. He didn't want her, for all the right reasons. And would be getting her, for all the wrong ones.

Jane hadn't doubted Mabel's diagnosis for a minute. Mabel was never wrong about maternity. All the mothers in the old neighborhood had come to her, before their own doctors. Mabel thought they had discussed it Friday, along with the demotion. Must have been after Jane had fallen asleep on her sofa. Oops.

Mabel just couldn't see that it really mattered. Why not just call Greg back upstairs and tell him she was pregnant, after all? she'd said.

Jane fervently wished that Greg would accept their explanation about the string of misunderstandings. But she couldn't bring herself to take the risk, not after humiliating him in the infants' department that morning. He'd initiated a showdown and she'd made a fool of him. Then he'd come to double-check on her condition after work and she'd turned him off again, insisting there was no baby. Then tonight, less than one hour ago, she'd shunned his marriage proposal with open outrage.

It took some doing, but Jane managed to explain the need for secrecy over the pregnancy. After all the twists and turns, Greg wouldn't buy the truth anymore. He would think that she'd been aware of the letter's contents all along.

She would absolutely die if he suspected her of deliberate entrapment all over again. But she did want her child to carry the Baron name. The baby was unquestionably a Baron and deserved a solid foundation, the security a marriage certificate would bring.

As he'd said himself, it wouldn't have to be forever. . . .

Naturally, with all the city officials crowding the makeshift chapel, a marriage license had been a mere formality. And Mabel and Clark were only more than happy to serve as their witnesses. The ceremony proceeded without a hitch. Within thirty minutes, Jane was Mrs. Gregory Baron, with the late Amanda's dazzling four-carat diamond ring on her finger to prove it.

Sir's eyes were the first to mist as the bridal couple turned around to hail their guests.

Jane laughed, in an excited, helpless sort of way. Undoubtedly, she'd be the last one crying—after Greg lived through the novelty of seeing his child enter the world. Then the reversion to the old ways would most likely begin. He'd return full-time to his California interests and she would be left holding the baby. All alone.

But this was no time to dwell on the realities of the future. This was her wedding day! And she needed to appear to get pregnant right before Greg's eyes. What had Sir said earlier about the timing? Something about fogging the events, so no one suspected the date of her conception.

She would have to use some of her father-in-law's outdated trickery—on her own husband!

The mayor and his wife were the last of the guests to clear out, shortly before midnight. Greg wound his arm around Jane in the foyer as Clark and Mabel stepped outside for a moment to see the guests off.

Greg's mouth lingered near her ear, his breath hot on her neck. "Come home with me, won't you?"

She tipped her face up to study her new husband. That he had to broach the question at all was so painful. But he didn't have a choice. How much would be for show was still up in the air. In his mind, anyway!

He mistook her silence for indecision. "Honey, I know it's preposterous that I have to ask, but—"

"Oh, it's preposterous any way you look at it," she lamented. "But yes, I will."

They smiled as their elders strolled back over the threshold, arm in arm.

"Wasn't that nice?" Mabel queried brightly.

"We did it, Mabel," Clark crowed, tweaking her cheek. "Most fun I've had in a long time, too."

Greg bared his teeth in frustration. What could be more dangerous than a steamrolling father with a fragile ticker? "You do like to be at the helm always, Sir."

Clark Baron chuckled in affirmation. "It is my nature, but I've always been more than willing to share all that is mine with you."

Sure, as long as Greg reflected Sir's every opinion!

"We'll be leaving now," Greg said. "Thank you so much for everything."

"Yes," Jane chimed in. "Thank you so much."

Grimes appeared in the foyer with the street clothes they'd arrived in and a sack containing some buffet leftovers.

"You've thought of everything," Greg marveled dryly, taking the bulk of the load.

"Not everything," Mabel lilted, raising a finger. "There're the little people to remember."

Jane gulped. Was her grandma so scattered that she was going to somehow give away her secret to Greg after all?

Grimes was the first to nod in real understanding. "Ah, yes. They're wrapping up the top layer of the cake for travel right now."

Jane slowly released a breath. "Oh, the china figurines," she clarified. "I didn't get it at first!"

Greg forced a grin. "Had me hookwinked, too." Hoodwinked and hog-tied. Within a block of a few hours, his whole future had been reshaped. Gregory Baron, a man who knew exactly what he wanted and exactly where he was going, had been abruptly cast adrift in a sea of unknowns.

"YOU'RE EATING THAT STUFF now?" Greg's large form loomed in the kitchen doorway of the condo an hour later, just as Jane was slicing a second wedge from the large circle of cake on the table. Even in the soft glow of the stove light he couldn't mistake the blue storm brewing in her eyes.

"I'm hungry," she complained, drawing her tongue around her chocolate-frosted lips.

"I thought that part was supposed to be frozen, saved for the first anniversary," he objected.

She gasped in open surprise. "I'm shocked that you know that!"

"I've been down this road before," he said in quiet reminder.

"So where is that other layer of yours?" she couldn't help snipping. "Sir's freezer?"

"We all ate it on the appropriate night, a long time ago."

She swallowed hard. "*We?*"

"You wouldn't have had a clue at the time. You were only six, and the bride and groom weren't on top of the cake anymore. Or together." His chest muscles tightened as he tensed. "I came back home on the weekend of what was to be my first anniversary. I needed my family, and all of you were there."

Her lashes swept her delicate cheeks. "Oh."

He heaved a breath, leaning deeper into the doorway. "Yeah, Dad's a royal pain sometimes, but he's never refused me a lifeline when I've needed it."

"Look, you've made it more than clear why you married me!" she lashed back. "You couldn't break Sir's heart. I know that. I get it."

"Janey, I—"

"And it doesn't have to be forever, either," she cried in interruption. "All your messages have been received!"

Greg winced, watching her turn his mother's impressive diamond ring on her slender finger. His rash proposal must have been hard to take right before the ceremony. Even though she'd always wanted him, he wasn't the right guy for her. He'd been determined to step aside so that Jane could have the kind of wedding night every woman deserved—complete with dreams of hearth and home. But despite his feelings on the subject, he was the groom after all. Her first, anyway. All the joy he'd always wished for Jane on her wedding night had ended up as his responsibility.

Fortunately, the one place he was certain to fulfill her was the bedroom. They were so comfortable with each other in the art of lovemaking. All the barriers magically fell off, then: age, temperament, career goals. They lost themselves in each other. In the deep feelings they shared.

He wanted to give her something to remember. A pleasurable memory that would overshadow all the disappointments of the day, of the circumstances.

But he didn't want to take another hasty step into hazardous territory. As much as he would have liked to scoop her up into his arms and haul her off to claim his husbandly rights, he'd made a painfully deliberate decision to slow down the pace. To prove his goodwill, he'd dug out the pajama bottoms he wore only on the coldest of Minnesota nights. His new bride apparently wasn't too troubled by such neutralities. While he was showering, she'd shucked down to her bra and panties right there in the kitchen. Her dress and veil were hanging carelessly over the teak wine rack in the corner.

It was probably the same childish way she'd treated the smaller version of that dress twenty years ago. But she wasn't a child any longer. She was a full-grown woman, with the sleekest limbs that had ever glided over his.

To Greg's own surprise, his gaze drifted back to what presently intrigued him most, her vulnerable expression.

She wasn't all she-cat, as he feared she might be. She was a lady full of churning emotions and open indecision.

And she was his bride.

Little Janey Haley was the new Mrs. Baron. Wearing his own mother's precious gemstone to give her position grounded reality. It had always been a symbol of stability to him. The woman who wore that ring would have to be strong, loyal and compassionate. He never could have imagined it on Nicole's finger. But it looked so dangerously right on Jane. Even if she was sucking a dab of fudgy frosting off it now as she plowed back into her cake.

No matter what happened, the ring was Jane's forever. A gut feeling told him so.

Jane watched his long strong fingers curl around the door-jamb, wondering if their marriage would last through the night, much less the year. Had she pushed him too far with her candid outburst? But it was what he would expect from her. A little sass and fire. It wasn't in her nature to crumble. Though for the first time in her life she felt like it. Pregnant, trapped in a marriage the groom considered inconvenient. It killed her inside that he didn't want her with the fervor expected on one's wedding night.

The bottom line was that whatever either of them expected or wanted didn't matter much. The baby's future had to be the first priority. She would have to learn lessons in tolerance and patience, refocus some of her self-centered energies toward her new role of mother. To begin with, she had to go through the motions of making a baby, lure Greg into her family nest.

"Care for some cake?" she asked with forced brightness.

"No, thanks. I'll freeze whatever's left. For whomever..."

She smiled between nibbles of cake. "Well, I just can't resist a treat set in front of me."

"You are a treat," he claimed in sudden seductive candor. "Your skin has never been more translucent. Your breasts never so ripe—" He paused with a frown. "Is it...your time...?"

"No!" And it wouldn't be for quite some time! Jane could feel the glow ooze to a red-hot flush. "Brides are supposed to be...glowing," she added in a stumble, feeling like she had a positive home pregnancy test result mounted on her head in place of her discarded wedding veil. She knew she sounded like a nervous virgin, at war with her own desires and fears. She was in an internal war, all right. She wanted him, needed him, but was too hurt and annoyed to let him off the hook just yet.

And he was frozen in his own mysterious uncertainties. He was hovering in the doorway like a tiger, his whipcord-lean body primed to spring.

Jane worked to quell the quiver of longing pulsing between her thighs as she surveyed his length with a raw hunger that no cake could begin to satisfy. Her gaze eventually centered on the shower-damp hair scoring his belly, arrowing down beneath the elastic band of his cotton pants.

"Like what you see?" he gently teased.

Jane averted her eyes and hands, toying with the fragile figurines from the cake top. "Do you know what the ceremony is supposed to mean?" she asked softly. "How important it is? What kind of commitments are involved?"

"I guess I reacted more than analyzed," he acquiesced.

"You should be grateful that I didn't storm out of your father's house!" she retorted in an emotional rush, squeezing the little groom's throat between her fingers.

"I am," he assured, his gaze on her as she choked his miniature counterpart to death. "In an effort to repay your cooperation, I'm trying to give you space, to understand where you're at right now."

"Well, I'm all mixed up," she confessed in a babble. "First you broke things off in some gallant move to free me up for all the young Minnesota males on the loose. I managed to survive that blow, salvaging my pride, going on with my job. Then you yanked away my job! I tried to right that wrong, only to have you accuse me of trying to trap you into marriage with a sham pregnancy. We finally cleared up all of that and now here we are, hitched! Legal and binding. For heaven only knows how long," she said, making the china couple dance on the tabletop with a tap-tap-tap.

"It's been a crazy cycle," he agreed gently.

He was making it so hard to maintain an irritated edge, and keep her secret, Jane inwardly griped. It was all she could do not to fly into his arms and tell him the whole truth, beg for his understanding.

But she wasn't up to the risk. He wouldn't want his child and he would never trust her again.

The whole thing simply wasn't fair. To her or their baby!

A sudden movement from Greg made her heart leap. But he was padding rather than pouncing, and on his way to the refrigerator.

"I could use a taste of that champagne Grimes sent along." He swung open the icebox door and pulled out a bottle by the neck. Without waiting for her response, he reached up into the cupboard and produced two stemmed glasses. Jane watched the action, one she'd seen dozens of times before. But she found herself taking a whole new look at the scant inventory of dishware on those shelves. As a guest she had never cared that the condo was sadly lacking in cooking utensils, and other household items in general. It had been rather enticing that the place was set up more like a bachelor's lair. Now, as a wife and expectant mother, she couldn't help thinking of all the things she used at her own apartment each and every day. Useful, necessary, boring things. Were they going to set up housekeeping? And if so, where?

"Greg, how are we going to live?" she asked bleakly. "Certain behavior will be expected. . . ."

Greg had popped the cork with practiced ease and was filling the glasses. "Well, I've been giving that some thought, and I'm hoping that you'll move in here. Being only blocks from the store takes away the commuting hassle . . ."

"And this place is far nicer than my suburban apartment," she finished on a defensive note.

"Yes." He slanted her a teasing look of apology from the counter. "I like to go first-class whenever possible."

"Okay," she agreed abruptly. *Our child deserves your best.*

Greg's forehead wrinkled in surprise over her compliance, but he didn't question it. With a flourish he brought the drinks to the table, easing down in the chair beside her. "You never did have a taste of this, did you, with Grimes feeding you ginger ale all night. What a crazy twist that you could've had it. Probably really could've used it."

Jane cast a wry look at the champagne, amused that the truth took a full circle back to the more appropriate ginger ale. She wouldn't dream of ingesting alcohol in her condition. But he was waiting, lifting his glass in a toast.

"To the future," he proclaimed, clinking his crystal against hers. She humored him by pressing the rim of her glass to her lips, pretending to take a taste.

They sat there together for a long space of time, recounting the ceremony and the cunning of their benefactors, slowly sinking into the comfort zone they'd shared as lifelong confidants.

Greg's erotic yearnings grew between sips of champagne and peeks at her scantily clad curves. Would she give him the chance to make the night shine? He'd just keep on feeding her the bubbly. She'd be his eager lover soon enough! Why, she hadn't squeezed the little groom's throat in over an hour's time.

As Greg consumed glass after glass of the sparkling drink, Jane worked secretly to recycle hers back into the bottle and into his glass. This was his second heavy dose of the night, so he was beginning to look a little bleary. Tipsy enough to take the distinct lipstick prints on her glass at face value, and her feigned tipsiness, as well. She'd let him win the seductive challenge, as soon he was nudged beyond birth-control concerns.

When Greg began to teeter in his chair shortly before three o'clock, she feared she'd played the game too long. With a coy grin she peeled off her underthings and drew the groom figure to her mouth, kissing his little head, licking the length of his painted-on tuxedo.

To her relief, Greg, though unsteady, still had the stamina to haul her into his lap. He tipped her back against his chest, pressing his fingers into her shoulders. Satisfied by the involuntary shudder that shook her, he began to knead her flesh with deep strokes. His large hands rotated over the smooth skin above her breasts, pouring fire over her entire chest. Her tender nipples grew hard, though he hadn't laid a finger on them.

His groan of satisfaction intermingled with hers.

He leaned into her ear, taking a long sucking pull of her lobe. "So, Mrs. Baron, are you interested in crossing the 'in name only' line tonight?"

Jane pressed her back against him, and then playfully covered her erect nipples with a dollop of the rich decorator's frosting. "I believe I forgot to feed the groom at the reception," she purred.

"You're an angel," he slurred. "And a witch." He turned her in his sinewy arms, arching her on his lap, capturing her frosted flesh in his mouth.

Jane gasped. The sensations zinging through her sensitive breast were a cross between pleasure and pain. She stiffened in his arms, raking his hair with trembling fingers.

"I don't ever want to hurt you, Janey," he rasped, burying his face in her softness.

"You're a very careful lover," she assured, sliding off the chair so she could tug at his pajama bottoms.

"That's not all I mean," he tried to explain, lifting his hips off the hard chair so she could undress him. "I mean your heart, too."

"Oh, Greg. Not now."

"Let's go to bed, honey."

He tried to rise, but she pushed him back in place.

"Please don't make me wait anymore," he pleaded, his desire in rock-solid evidence.

"I won't." Bracing the heels of her hands on his shoulders, Jane swung one leg over his lap so that she was straddling him. Ever so slowly she sat down on his erection, pocketing him in her moist intimate tunnel.

He released a hungry guttural sound as she moved over him, slowly, then rapidly. Soon they were lost in the sensations of sizzling friction caused by her wild piloting. Reveling in her assertiveness, he grasped her breasts in his large hands, drawing the tips of her nipples over his hair-roughened chest, sending more lightning through her system.

It was soon over in a hot frenzied rush. Jane crumpled, locking her limbs around him so they wouldn't topple over.

"Looks like we made it," he mumbled in disbelief. "Right in here . . ."

And right in time, she thought, raking back the golden hair on his forehead. Now, when she told him he was a father, he'd have real reason to believe it happened tonight.

JANE AWOKE TUESDAY morning in Greg's bed to find sunlight slanting through the window at an angle that suggested mid-morning. She bolted up in bed, and blinked at the clock radio on the nightstand. It was ten-thirty!

And she was alone in the king-size bed, dressed in one of his T-shirts.

Where was Greg? Was the wedding bit all a crazy dream? She'd just about convinced herself that it had all been a nocturnal movie of the mind, when she spied the wedding dress draped over a reading chair.

Relief poured over her. Everything was legal. Far from ideal, but legit just the same. Which meant she had a fighting chance for her child.

Jane swung her legs over the side of the bed, finding that she was feeling a little woozy. Part of her condition, no doubt. Along with the headaches and unsettled stomach she'd been living with lately. She moved into the master bathroom to freshen up, touched to find a fresh bath towel and some new toiletries waiting for her. She'd cleared out all of her things when they'd broken up. How thoughtful. No, she amended in horror. How diabolical! It meant he'd had them on hand, for a new conquest!

She thought about Greg's footloose life-style as she showered, wondering what their stifling vows would mean to him. Would he be willing to play the faithful husband under the circumstances?

Of course he would! she decided by the time she was drying herself.

Jane again donned the large white T-shirt and ventured into the hallway leading to the front of the condo. As she neared the living room, she could hear Greg's voice, presumably on the telephone. She froze as the voice grew harsh.

"It was impulsive, Nik. Yeah, I know I was just there the other day. But this whole thing fell together overnight. The timing was right for us. That's what matters."

Jane leaned into the rough plaster wall, a knife slicing through her unsettled stomach. He was already on the phone to his ex-wife! Before he'd even said good-morning to her, he was bringing Nicole up to speed. Jane couldn't help but wonder how close the pair was after nearly two decades and a divorce between them.

"You've known all along how I feel about Jane," he went on.

Jane hugged her arms into her chest. She doubted Greg himself even knew how he felt about her. One thing they all did know, however, was that Nicole was still quite possessive of her ex. She hadn't found anyone, so she didn't want Greg to settle down, either. Jane hadn't seen Nicole since the ill-fated wedding in 1975, but the static lived on. A little reading between the lines over the years had convinced her that Nicole didn't like Greg to return home for any reason.

And now he had a real tie to keep him at this end. Matrimony. To the little flower girl who had predicted doom to their union.

His hoot sliced the air. "No, I'm sure Janey didn't put a voodoo spell on me. Not then or now! Everybody's been buzzing around here, thrilled out of their heads. No, Dad made the arrangements—under my direction," he hastily added.

Jane bit her lip. His storytelling technique showed signs of strain. Would he break down, tell Nicole it was a temporary arrangement? They'd agreed to tell no one. She listened on with a thudding heart.

"If I sound annoyed, it's because of your cross-examination and no other reason." He listened for a moment, his voice dropping a note. "Of course we'll have to put a stop to that facet of our friendship. I am an honorable man."

Jane's eyes widened in alarm. He was still going to bed with his ex-wife! Such a thing had never occurred to her during their three-month romance. If she didn't cut off this conversation, he was going to spill something she didn't want to know. With a fortifying breath she launched herself into the living room.

Greg, lounging on the sofa in navy briefs with a cordless phone to his ear, started as she came into his vision. "Look, just tend to business as expected," he directed in abrupt dismissal. "Bye." He ran a thumb over the disconnect button, easing up into a seated position on the cushions. "Good morning," he ventured guardedly. "Guess you really overdid it on the bubbly last night."

She shrugged beneath the baggy shirt. "Yeah, I suppose. I think you would've fed it to me through a hose, given the chance."

His dancing eyes crinkled at the corners in a way she'd always found irresistible. "Well, I just wanted you to loosen up."

"Cooperate, you mean."

"I think we've always been mutually cooperative," he asserted smoothly.

"Been busy on the phone, I see," she said, strolling closer.

"Yeah, yeah," he replied briskly, setting the handset back in its charger on the glass-topped table. "Dad sends his congratulations to you. Wants us to take the day off."

She didn't doubt that Greg had spoken to Sir, but it had to have been earlier on. He didn't realize that she'd heard a word of his last exchange, and she wasn't about to volunteer the truth.

"Ah, the whole day off," she mockingly rejoiced, placing a hand on her hip. "Honeymoon of my dreams."

Greg watched the hem of his own T-shirt creep up over the curve of her bottom, and briefly envisioned a proper honeymoon himself. "It would be feasible to schedule a trip sometime in the future. Maybe a Caribbean cruise this fall.

"I spoke to Dad's physician, Dr. Crane, this morning after his house call to the estate. Our marriage has lifted Sir's spirits to wondrous heights, but he isn't ready to fully take over the helm again just yet."

"I wasn't suggesting we run off," Jane returned indignantly. "That was a beastly conclusion to jump to!"

"This isn't the morning-after scene I'd envisioned at all," he complained. He crooked his mouth and his finger. "Come over here and sit beside me." When she bristled under his amorous gaze, he chuckled. "Believe me, you'll be safer if you do. You're downright irresistible in that pose."

With a huff and a tug on her shirt, she marched over and sat down.

"I shouldn't have jumped to that unfair honeymoon conclusion," he admitted mildly. When he made a move to touch her bare knee, she clamped her legs together. He withdrew with a sharp breath.

"You know Sir's health is on my mind, too!" she scolded. It was plain that if Greg could run off for a couple of weeks, it would be an extra trip back to L.A., not a honeymoon. She felt uncharacteristically helpless on that score. And it brought out the worst in her.

"Some issues won't wait," he forged on with firmness. "I know precious little about pregnancy, Jane—"

She turned to glare at him. "What do you mean?"

"How much time do we have?" he impatiently clarified. "Before you'll be expected to show?"

Jane folded her arms across her middle in a maternal move to conceal the life inside her. "It depends. On heredity, the physical condition of the mother. Young athletic women can go on for months without showing. The process starts with a little plumpness in the chest and belly."

His golden brows narrowed. "I figure Dad really doesn't know much about it, either. And the pretense is for his benefit alone. Tricking him for the time being is bound to be easy. But it's going to be so damn tough to correct him!"

"Too many unprotected nights like last night and you won't have to bother," she couldn't resist gibing with wicked glee.

He cleared his throat, angling an arm behind the sofa back. "Good point. That can't happen again, honey. We've got to be more careful from now on."

She shot him a withering look. "You're in overdrive with all these assumptions of yours."

Greg balked, amazed by the extent of her bad temper. Things had been fine when they'd retired last night. He'd been high on drink, but he remembered their afterglow cuddle in bed. "I hope that as long as we are married, you'll want to behave like any married couple," he proposed, fingering the damp tendrils of hair near her temples.

"Like you and Nicole still behave?" she blurted out angrily.

"Ah, so you did hear me on the line," he said with new understanding. "That's why I'm in hot water so soon."

"So tell me, Greg, just how do you intend to fit that paratrooper of a woman into our little love nest?"

7

GREG GRITTED HIS TEETH. If only he could make light of this. Nicole had lost her hold on him years ago. In her finest hour she couldn't have held a candle to Jane. But if he put it that way to this impassioned spitfire, she might think him capable of making her happy for the long haul.

"Nicole's no paratrooper," he teased lamely. "She's afraid of heights."

"Well, she wouldn't have to scale too high to leap into this situation," Jane cried back in accusation.

"Honey, my ties to Nicole are thread thin. We have our own separate lives outside the production company."

"Then why were you explaining things to her?"

"Because she and Kevin are business partners and friends. If he'd answered the office phone, I would have told him. You know there are bound to be all sorts of facets coming into play here. We're merging our lives, for pete's sake!"

"Well, I'm keeping most of my belongings at my apartment," Jane declared in a sudden wave of self-preservation. "We may desire our own space overnight from time to time. No one need be the wiser."

Greg had the grace to express his pained surprise. "What for?"

"I don't know, yet," she retorted with a petulant lift of her small chin. "What if one of your California girls breezes into town and you want to play the merry bachelor?"

Greg curled his fist in frustration, then got the better of his passions, taking her slender pale hand in his. "I will be true to you, just as I vowed to do."

"And will Nicole understand?"

"Nicole is history!" he ground out.

"Liar!" she cried. "Sex keeps a relationship right up-to-date. It's about as current as you can get!"

"Janey, at twenty-five you surely understand about old relationships. Old lovers who . . . well, get together to satisfy their needs."

"I do understand, in theory," she admitted. "But not with you!"

"I don't plan to seek out her company," Greg thundered. "You and I are a team, a married couple."

"Did you and Nicole, ah, do it after we started doing it?"

"You mean after Christmas?" He couldn't help smiling. "You really are crazy for me, aren't you?"

"You arrogant monster!" Her fist came flying at his chest. He snagged it just in time to ward off a blow.

"Janey! I was only teasing, trying to lighten you up!"

She wrenched free, shooting up from the sofa.

"Since when can't you take a joke?" He looked up at her in helpless fury. "You've always been excitable, but you've really gone overboard. With your transfer, with our relationship. It's like nitroglycerin is flowing through your veins!"

"I'm going over to the store," she announced with a sniff.

"That's nuts. What will people think?"

"Everyone will understand that we couldn't just jet off and leave Sir. Besides, who'll even see me in the Bargain Basement?" she challenged.

"Your station has changed," he swiftly differed. "You're part of the Baron family now. There is a certain line drawn between us and them."

"Meaning?"

"Meaning that you don't belong in the basement anymore!"

"I'll happily take on a managerial position," she crowed. "Put me in charge of Toys."

He groaned. "Let's not get started on the Nibling issue again."

"Then make room for me elsewhere."

"There really aren't any open positions. You wouldn't want me to give someone the chop to make room for you, would you?"

"No! But you know I'm not the type to sit around."

"Dad does assume you'll be retiring. So maybe, just for now, you could—"

"Even if I were pregnant, I'd want to be more than the Baron incubator!"

"Dad is a traditionalist on family life, just as he is with Emporium policy. He's going to have trouble with your reasoning," he predicted. "But on the other hand, you can't seem to do any wrong in his eyes."

She whirled on her heel and started for the hallway.

"Will you at least give me time to think of some sort of worthy title for you?"

"No, damn you!" she turned back to cry. "You had your chance to overrule Nibling's decision to turn me out of Toys. You had the chance to marry me of your own free will. As it is, you took the jerk's way out of everything."

"That isn't fair!"

"Well, let me put it to you this way—I have spent a lot of my valuable time plotting a better Bargain Basement, and by golly, I'm going to revamp that cellar if it's the last thing I do!"

"But you don't have to anymore!" he called after her. "Would it help you to know that I haven't touched Nicole since Thanksgiving?"

Her voice was hollow, distant and bitter as it echoed back down the hallway. "You could've saved yourself a lot of trouble by telling me that in the first place. But, oh, no, you just had to be courted, cajoled, fought over."

"You did all of that wonderful stuff to me?" he hollered back. "Just now? While I was in my underwear?"

"Yes!"

He scratched his head, grumbling. "How'd I miss that kind of treatment?"

Greg paused for an indecisive moment, then decided to trail after his bride. He found her in the bedroom, leaning over the boldly striped bedspread, rummaging through the tote holding last night's clothing. Judging by the moon she was flashing at the doorway, she was obviously unaware of his proximity.

"Did you hear my question?" he asked calmly.

She snapped to rigid attention, turning to glare at his large hair-dusted body, fluid against the doorframe. "Sure, I know how you missed the good stuff. You're a bonehead!"

"Janey," he cautioned in a dangerously silky voice. "I'm getting ticked."

"Tough."

Greg strode up to the bed, grabbed the tote from her hands and flung it to the plush gray carpeting. "You aren't going anywhere today."

"I will if I want to! You can't force me—"

Jane's objection was cut off by Greg clamping his mouth directly over hers. She absorbed the pressure of his firm lips with a steely resolve, attempting to fight the tantalizing burn of his roaming tongue. She tried to squirm free before reason was gone, but his hands, positioned on her neck and her spine, held her hard and fast. She soon stopped fighting it. Her softness against his hardness was an unbeatable combination. As always, she began a steady melt into his heat, like an ice cube on hot asphalt.

He made certain she was limp with longing before he turned her loose.

"Force never has been and never will be an issue between us, Janey."

Jane lifted her eyes to his silvered ones. "Touché," she conceded breathlessly. "I can't say no to you, and we both know it."

"I just want things to be as they've always been between us," he confided. "It would be a shame not to continue on with our natural closeness, now, of all times."

He knew so little of the times he was talking about, she thought with a pinch of pain. She ached to tell him the truth, but he was so obviously on the edge of reason already.

"I think my mistake has been in assuming that you are totally secure all of the time," he confessed in apology. "You've always seemed so sure of yourself, not particularly affected by Nicole's presence in my office. She's always been leery of you, jealous of my affection for you. Guess I took your good nature for granted concerning her."

"I shouldn't have lost my cool so quickly," she relented. "But to wake up the morning after our wedding and catch you on the phone with your ex-wife...it was too much. Then you avoided telling me...." She trailed off, her lovely features crumpled in hurt.

"I brushed off the call only because it was inconsequential," he hastily assured. "We're a united force to the world, honey. Nicole has no place in our relationship."

Jane was sure Nicole would be nothing but trouble, but decided not to argue the issue further. "I really don't want to go in today, Greg," she admitted. "You're right about it being bad for appearances. I imagine the situation looks odd enough to the staff as it is."

"I did make some plans for us," he ventured.

"Oh?" Her system hummed under his lazy lover's look.

"Well, we did fall asleep on the finest of terms last night, so I figured it would be a safe bet."

She drew a coy smile. "So what's on your agenda?"

"This morning will include a little nap, then brunch delivered from Casey's Grill down the street. We'll stop by your apartment this afternoon and pack up some of your gear. Then it's off to my father's house for dinner and the opening of our wedding gifts. Your car is still over there, so we can use both our vehicles to haul the loot back here."

"In all the excitement, I'd forgotten about the gifts," she admitted sheepishly.

"I'll take that as a compliment!" he said roguishly, dipping his head to nibble at her throat.

"I don't suppose there'll be anything useful in that mountain of stuff," she said in disappointment.

"Nope. You'll just have to get accustomed to going out and buying the useful things you need. Without concerning yourself with the price tag."

"It will be different, after being raised to budget every penny, clip every coupon."

"Mabel went overboard with her lessons in thrift," he confided. "Dad has laid a pile of dough on her over the years. There's no romantic interest there, I'm sure, but there certainly is a loving bond."

"She never let on to me that she's well-off," Jane huffed.

"She probably didn't want to spoil you. Wanted to save the privilege for me."

"Well, you're lacking some very important items around here," she complained.

"The hell I am!" he growled in protest.

Jane inhaled as Greg clamped her bottom with his long strong fingers, pressing her in to his swollen penis. "Hey, I already know nothing's lacking down there," she teased. "But there's more to marriage than that!"

"Not right now there isn't."

Jane couldn't help but agree as she saw her own desires mirrored in his silvered gaze.

As she wound her arms around his neck to snuggle closer, he eased the baggy T-shirt over her head. His hands glided down the curve of her back, then up and around to her lush breasts, weighing their heaviness with a ravenous groan. She moaned in soft harmony, suddenly wanting to make herself eternally irresistible to this man who had sparked a whole new life inside her.

With a sweeping motion, Greg eased her off her feet and onto the rumpled maroon bed covers. She landed flat on her back, her loose wavy hair fanning her shoulders. Propping his hands on the mattress over her head, he hovered with a reverent wonder.

She fluttered her lashes to hide a flicker of disappointment. Why couldn't he simply accept that they were bonded forever?

He would. Given time, given proof.

Her blue eyes gleamed with a fresh, coy determination as she reached up and inched his skimpy briefs over his hips and down his sinewy legs. He kicked the scrap of cotton out of the way and bent down to shower kisses in the valley of her rib cage, down lower to her navel, and the small nest of hair at her juncture. He inhaled her scent with bold pleasure, backing up on his knees to explore her secret opening with his fingers.

She cried out in delight as he kissed and stroked her, bringing her to an electrifying plane of arousal. He was openly surprised at her swift soar, but when did Janey ever really make sense to him?

Jane was determined to make the best of her ultrasensitive condition. Just as she intended to take pleasure in nurturing the life inside her. Pregnancy was supposed to be a joyous time, and as with everything else, she would get the most out of it, make it an adventure.

Greg eased inside her, bringing her to a speedy orgasm that amazed them both. They then took a more leisurely route to climax, indulging in a slow rhythmic journey of exploration and experimentation.

Spent and content, Greg cuddled Jane to his chest, leisurely pondering the issues of commitment, security and real love. It was difficult to imagine any new husband feeling more fulfilled than he did right now. He couldn't help wondering, for the first time ever, if maybe this truly was meant to be his happy ending, after all. Did an old cynical bachelor like himself deserve this sort of security at the crossroads of his life? More important, did a young fresh spirit like Jane deserve to be chained to him?

She did actually want him, though, he thought in comfort. It was remarkable how focused she'd remained on that point over the years. It was so important that he not disappoint her. No matter what happened, he would have to handle her heart with the utmost care. Hell, maybe she did know what was best for both of them.

Jane purred like a kitten as she burrowed against him. He in turn buried his face in her thick fragrant hair.

"It's going to be all right, honey," he rasped to her dozing form. "You're the greatest treasure a man could ever wish for, and I'm not going to blow this opportunity."

The sound of his voice in the stillness jarred Jane awake. She fought to hold her features placid, as though still in slumber. A difficult feat, when in fact she'd never felt more awake or alive! Greg was obviously making the comforting promise to himself, and might be embarrassed to learn that she'd overheard him. Thanks heavens she had! It was the perfect wedding gift, his genuine vow of dedication. Even the most thought-out marriages couldn't begin with a better guarantee than that!

JANE WASN'T LOOKING for familiar faces as she crossed the lobby of the Medical Arts Building on that first Tuesday in May. She'd slipped out of the Emporium and across the street on the pretense of catching lunch, when in reality she was having her fluctuating blood pressure double-checked by her ob-gyn, Gail Gilbertson. Gail had been her doctor for eight years, monitoring her erratic menstrual cycle with keen concern throughout the course of that time. Jane had poured her heart out to the likable physician during her initial checkup right after the wedding last month, imposing on the confidentiality of the doctor-patient relationship. Gail preferred to include expectant fathers in all phases of the pregnancy, including the exams, but reluctantly agreed to help Jane through the ordeal. On the condition that she consider telling Greg the truth about the date of conception, and calm down enough to bring her pressure back to normal. The good doctor was convinced that solving the husband problem would automatically solve the health problem.

Jane desperately wanted to do so. But the risk still seemed far too great. If Greg didn't have a second life to escape to, it wouldn't be so bad. But unlike the majority of the world's male population, Greg Baron did have an alternative home base across the country. One full of exciting challenges.

If he thought she'd been playing him for a patsy all this time, he'd no doubt find all the more reason to retreat back to his safer world in Los Angeles. With Nicole in the background. And despite all his protestations, Jane believed that Greg would absolutely love being a father. That he was all wrong in his fears about being too old or incapable of settling down.

If only he could see this as his chance to fulfill himself!

Jane barreled out of the building's swinging glass doors eager to lose herself in the noon-hour crush on the busy sidewalk. She was so intent on distancing herself from the telltale building that she blindly ran into none other than the proud grandpapa-to-be, Clark Baron.

"Janey, dear!" he greeted. "What a splendid surprise!"

"Yes," she agreed breathlessly, smoothing her peach dress against the wind as she advanced on the elder Baron and Grimes. "How are you feeling?"

"Oh, drained and irritated from a battery of tests," he grumbled, his busy silver brows knifing together over his nose.

"Necessary tests," Grimes inserted mildly, gazing off into the blue sky.

"So what brings you to the Medical Arts?" The moment the query was out of Sir's mouth, he brightened with his own answer. "Oh, of course," he murmured. "The baby doctor."

Jane smiled shyly. "Uh-huh."

Sir squeezed her hand in his. "First appointment," he assumed. "How exciting. So when is the child expected?"

Jane inhaled with a frozen smile. She had to keep her charade straight. Sir was to be given the real due date, for he had believed her to be pregnant all along and Greg was to be fed a bogus date coinciding with a wedding-night conception. Being that first babies could be unpredictable, she hoped her child would be clever enough to arrive someplace in the middle. "Second half of November was as close as she could come," she reported.

"She? A lady?" Sir was insultingly flabbergasted, obviously more interested in the sex of the doctor, than he was in her inconclusive prediction of the birth.

Jane smiled. Women in the workplace was an issue hot in her mind these days, so she welcomed the discussion.

"Gail Gilbertson's more than capable, Sir," she assured. "She's been practicing for fifteen years. And been my doctor for half of that time."

"I think I'd like to speak to her," Sir decided with pursed lips.

"I think not," Grimes interceded smoothly. "Jane and Greg can handle these personal details. You have enough to keep up your end, with easing back into the saddle at the store, building your strength to see this child into the world."

"Hell, I'm gonna live, you old pest," Sir retorted, taking Jane's elbow as the light turned green.

"There's more to life than breathing and bitching, Sir," Grimes pressed pleasantly. "You might want to play a bit of badminton with the tyke in a few years."

"Ha, that boy will have a baseball bat in his hand before he can talk!"

"Girls can play all the games with just as much skill as the boys," Jane chimed in on a teasing note.

"I will love a girl just as much," Sir declared gruffly. "Too much if she's just like you."

"His overall attitude has improved since finally getting you into the family, Jane," Grimes cut in to report. "But he still complains too much about these appointments of his."

"Torture!" Sir corrected on a bellow as they took the curb in front of his gray stone building. "They run me on a treadmill like a workhorse in the field, stick me with needles, hook me up to machines. Bah."

"I have just the thing to take your mind off your morning," Jane lilted, kissing his cheek.

His grimace softened. "I know. The baby."

"We'll have years to enjoy the baby," she protested, wiping the smudge of lipstick she left on his shallow cheek. "It's the store I want to speak to you about. In particular, the Bargain Basement."

He reared back. "But you're not down there anymore!"

"Of course I am," she said matter-of-factly. "And you should be glad."

"Why?"

"Because I'm turning it into a moneymaking operation, that's why!"

Sir made a sputtering sound. Grimes leaned over, as though to have a private word. "You've got to calm down. Expectant mothers can't take much strain."

Jane turned toward the traffic to conceal her grin. How clever of Grimes to divert Sir's attention from his own frailties. *Be strong for Janey.* And Sir did appear stronger. He'd been making steady progress since the wedding, dropping in at the store every few days. It was about time he found out she was still working right under his nose.

"C'mon now, you old fuddy-duddy," she said, playfully tugging him through the entrance. "I have something wonderful to show you."

They entered one of the elevators. Sir directed the uniformed operator to the bottom.

"Nobody told me you were still around here," he grumbled to Jane. "Why, I assumed you were settling into your new homemaking responsibilities."

"I'll be setting things up right along," Jane assured.

"Why not just take the easy route?" he implored in confusion.

"I am happy working in the store," she insisted, groping for the handrail as the elevator swooped down.

He raised a bony finger. "You're dizzy."

She rolled her eyes. "You've been saying that for twenty years!"

Moments later the doors swooshed open on the building's lowest level.

"You are going to love my surprise," she intoned, smoothing the dove-gray lapel of his suit jacket.

"If you've gotten that chunky manager of yours to do a lick of work I might get a little dizzy myself," he retorted.

Jane balked at him as they walked around the escalators toward the center counter. "If you've known about her habits all along, why..."

"Why have I kept her on?" He kept walking, but his voice dropped a note. "Because her late husband, Fred Pallack, served in the Korean War with me and went on to be one of the best salesmen Haberdashery has ever known. When he lay dying of cancer eighteen years ago, he asked me to watch over Audrey, give her a job. Oh, I know it's more like charity." He shrugged. "That's all it is, really. She's always been the lazy sort, so the basement seemed just right. She manages to keep the status quo down here, training personnel in the basics. I expect nothing more."

Jane smiled. "Well, a little change, a little challenge never hurt anybody."

Sir pulled his mouth tight to quell the protest on his lips. Jane noticed he'd been doing that a lot. She actually found that she missed his penchant for protest, his verbal sparring.

But for the time being, his complacency could be most useful. Sir would never be more flexible concerning her plans for the store than he would be for the next several months. By the time the baby was born, the Emporium might again be an innovator in downtown merchandising.

Just as Jane hoped, Audrey was in top form, waiting on three customers at once with the help of some part-time high school girls.

"I'll be damned," he uttered under his breath as Audrey shifted her girth to and fro beneath a snug purple nylon dress, as she rounded the counter to collect a variety of summer hats from different shelves. "Well, well, Audrey," Clark Baron greeted in open surprise.

She paused, patting her huge orange hairdo. "Oh, good afternoon, Sir."

Jane stepped in by the register to streamline the sales. She inadvertently drew Sir's attention to what they were buying. Mid-quality merchandise at modest prices. Something the Emporium had never sold before. It had always been junk for the basement and top of the line for all the departments above, with nothing in between.

Once the customers moved on with their slate-colored Baron's sacks, Audrey sent the young clerks to lunch. "So what do you think of it all?" she asked, excitedly sweeping the department with a large, freckled arm.

Sir followed her gesture with a keen eye. "What's happened here, Audrey?"

"Well, it's all due to Jane!"

"No, we did it together," Jane quickly assured.

"But you started it all!" Audrey insisted.

"Well, yes, I did come up with the initial scheme to sell necessities at reasonable prices. You see, Sir, the average worker downtown has a hard time finding small gifts, tissues, toilet paper, single-serve bottles of juice."

"Not to mention deodorant, aspirin, antacids," Audrey added.

"You can get some of these things, of course, but at prices far above the suburban discount stores where many of the workers do most of their leisure-hours shopping."

Sir stroked his chin. "Ah, so you're giving them what they need at the prices they're accustomed to paying."

"Exactly!" the ladies chorused.

"What are those?" Sir demanded, gesturing to a rack of clear tote bags emblazoned with the Baron name.

"I ordered those for the customers, so they can cart around their selections while they browse."

"There are a lot of smaller items down here, and it's difficult to carry them in your hands," Audrey put in.

"Reminds me of the old plastic baskets the dime stores used to have," he murmured with a shrug. "Clever."

"It will take some time to turn a profit, of course," Jane went on to admit. "And we'll have to experiment with the merchandise, figure out what moves."

Sir's mouth tightened again.

"How inventive," Grimes congratulated in support. "Isn't the mother of your grandchild clever."

A hush fell over the group.

"You're pregnant?" Audrey gasped in delight. "How wonderful."

"I thought everyone knew," Grimes faltered in apology.

"No harm done," Sir assured. "It's brand-new news, Audrey. Jane was just to the doctor and has managed to provide me with the beginnings of an heir."

"Due when?" Audrey eagerly demanded.

"Right around Christmas," Sir swiftly went on to lie, giving the store's nosiest Parker the date Jane planned to give Greg. Jane was happy enough. Audrey was considered an impeccable source. When she spread the news, as she would, people would believe it to be the true due date.

Audrey gave Jane a brief squeeze. "I don't know how you'll think of anything else!"

"I have plenty of energy and interest left over for the store," Jane assured.

"Me, too," Sir grumbled, looking around again. "And I imagine this is really costing me."

"Naturally there's some expense," Jane said stubbornly.

"I prefer to do some market analysis before I make a move so daring," he complained.

"The miniskirt analysis back in the sixties was timely," Grimes smoothly intoned.

"That wasn't the last decision made!"

Grimes rocked on his well-polished shoes. "No, there were the clogs of the seventies. You compiled projected sales, then ignored them, saying that nobody could possibly balance on the blasted things and would sue the store for all it's worth."

"Well, anyone can misjudge a trend," Sir blustered to his man, turning back to Jane. "How did you manage to get authorization for the buying?"

Audrey flushed with an injured look. "Why, I've had that authorization for years! I run the basement!"

"Yes, well, you can't blame me for forgetting your privileges," he grumbled. "You've rarely exercised them."

"Things are going to be different from now on," Audrey assured with a sound nod. "I like Jane's ideas and her pep. Hasn't been a boring moment since we got crackin' on this scheme."

"She even took the TV back to Appliances," Jane proudly announced, causing Sir's brow to lift in consternation and Audrey's apple cheeks to redden all the more.

He was about to expound on the issue when Greg appeared on the "Down" escalator.

"Little Sir!" Audrey swiftly welcomed, obviously hoping for a shift in subject. She rounded the counter, gliding up to offer her plump hand to him. "Congratulations on your new little addition."

Greg smiled blankly, looking anything but small in his crisp beige suit. "My what?"

"The baby, of course! How nice for you and Jane. How nice for the Baron family."

Greg's expression was murderous as he singled out his bride.

"Maybe I should acquaint Sir with the stock we've acquired," Jane interjected brightly. "Would you like to go see the stock, too, Greg?"

"More than I can say." With a firm hand on both his father and his wife, Greg steered them toward the curtained door marked Employees Only. Looking back, he noted that Grimes had lured the store's most gossipy employee over to a rack of sunglasses. He protected the family like a sentry when the need arose.

"Sir caught me coming out of the Medical Arts Building, darling." Jane sought to explain as Sir inspected the boxes of merchandise on the floor.

Greg's jaw sagged. "What were you doing over there?"

"She was seeing the baby doctor, you dense oaf," Sir barked. "What's this crate contain, Janey?"

"Oh, a new line of soap. Hypoallergenic. You'd be amazed at how many people are allergic to scent," she said, avoiding Greg's astonished look. "I took the liberty of isolating all the scented items, discontinuing some of the worst."

"In my day they just blew their damn noses," Sir grumbled.

"That particular one is a hot seller already," she promptly added.

"Really?" he asked on a brighter note.

"The line costs far less than the sort sold at the traditional cosmetic counters."

He stooped over the crate and extracted a bar. "I'll be . . ."

"Dad," Greg began, striding up to the silver-haired man with the soap under his nose.

Sir whirled to shove the soap in his son's face. "Smell this."

Greg turned his face. "It has no smell."

Sir took another sniff himself. "I'll be . . ."

"Father," Greg beseeched with clenched fists. "I thought we were going to postpone the pregnancy announcement."

"Ah, Grimes did it. You know how excitable he is."

"Grimey excitable?"

"Well, he usually keeps the excitement in. But he's so pleased with this blessed event that he lost his composure." Sir shrugged. "Guess it doesn't matter too much, now that you've been married for several weeks. It makes the child presumably legitimate. I did some quick calculating to come up with a respectable due date to appease the store busy-body," he consoled. "Aligned the forecasted birth within the boundaries of your marriage. It will stop some of the nastier gossipers," he turned to tell Jane.

"You handled it well," she congratulated.

"Just what are these dates?" Greg asked with strained modulation.

"The doctor has informed Jane that the genuine one is in mid-November," Sir supplied impatiently. "The one in sync with your wedding night would be closer to the Christmas mark."

"I see," Greg said tightly, wedging a finger beneath the knot of his forest-green tie as it tightened around his neck.

"Say, boy, you think you can spare our girl this afternoon?"

"I would like her all to myself," Greg protested silkily. "If I didn't have a meeting with the bank, I'd be tempted to take her home right this instant."

"Well, I want to take her to lunch," Sir informed them with a pat to Jane's arm. "We have so much to discuss. About the store, about the baby."

"By all means, take her," Greg invited. Jane fought a flinch as his roughened index finger grazed her cheek. "Just have her home by dinnertime."

8

GREG WAS A WRECK all afternoon. How could she have let this charade go public? And what had she been doing over at the Medical Arts Building?

He was on the verge of explosion by the time she waltzed into the condo at five-thirty.

"I am beat!" she proclaimed, bouncing onto the tweed-covered sofa.

"I don't doubt it!" he thundered, hovering over her in a combination of perplexity and outrage. "What the hell were you up to today?"

Jane kicked off her shoes, drew her feet up on the cushion, and began to rub her toes. "Well, the trouble started when your Dad caught me over at the medical building."

He threw his hands over his head. "You were really over there!"

"I didn't expect anybody to see me," she babbled defensively. "It was during the noon-hour rush. The sidewalks were teeming with workers. Anyhow, I was running a little late and I literally collided with Sir and Grimes."

"Why, Janey, why?"

"Why was I there? Because I had a bona fide doctor's appointment."

"And Dad jumped to the conclusion that it was concerning the baby!" he concluded. He paced as he absorbed the scene. "Couldn't you have simply told him you were having a wart removed?"

"He'd have wanted to see the sore spot—"

"You're quick," he interrupted, dropping down beside her feet. "You could've claimed it was on the bottom of one of these little babies."

She squealed when he pinched her little toe. "He's been patient for a due date for so long already," she reminded. "The home pregnancy-test claim, the doctor's-appointment backlog . . . well, it was bound to catch up with us."

"But if you'd have just told him the truth about your appointment," he sought to explain. "We could've roped him into keeping the secret a little longer."

"I wasn't quick enough," Jane admitted feebly. "Quick enough to think of a way to camouflage the truth."

"What!"

"Greg, I really was at my gynecologist's," she confessed. "I was feeling a little queasy, and it's fairly close to my usual yearly examination. So I just went in."

His eyes flinted. "You mean . . ."

"Yeah," she said sheepishly. "I really am pregnant."

"*Pregnant?*" He lunged back to his feet. "*You can't be!*"

"But I am, honey." Jane sat very still on the sofa, watching him from beneath her lashes.

Greg prowled across the room to the portable bar near the kitchen and poured himself two fingers of Scotch.

"I know it's a shock—"

"Oh, I don't know," he interrupted, corking the bottle. "This is the second time I've had to deal with the idea. A familiar numbness is already traveling up my spine."

"I'm sure it'll take some getting used to, just the same," she ventured to console.

"I, ah, need a breath of fresh air," he declared rather dazedly. He slid open the glass door leading to the balcony, sending the cool night air flooding inside.

"Don't stand too close to the edge out there," she teased awkwardly.

"I think it's too late to worry about taking a fall," he said before disappearing from view.

She gave him some solitary time, resting uneasily in the quiet chilly living room. Of course this twist was bound to be a shock, but couldn't he be more gracious about it? Her fragile feelings were crumbling into dust. Her life was taking a dream course, but it was far from fulfilling its promise. She was in the right place at the right time with the right man.

And it seemed to be all wrong in his mind.

He eventually returned, securing the door again. "Sorry, I left that open," he mumbled.

She lurched forward on the cushions with a gasp of dismay. "That's all you can say?"

"Well, I mean, with your condition and all . . ." He trailed off helplessly, freshening his drink at the bar. "So you figure this happened on our wedding night, then?" he asked, struggling for a controlled tone.

"Well," she hedged, "we were careless."

He took a large slurp of whiskey. It was a hot and scalding chaser to the cool night air. "So this means that Sir's dates are flip-flopped," he reasoned. "He thinks you're due in November and you're really due around the end of the year."

She nodded, hating the lie more and more. She wanted to take Dr. Gilbertson's advice and set him straight, admit that they'd started this child way back in February. But Greg was in no condition to accept it.

Oh, she cringed to think of how angry he'd be in the future, if and when he discovered that Sir had had the real scoop all along through Mabel's letter, and therefore had the dates straight.

"I hope you don't think I got pregnant deliberately."

He whirled her way suddenly with a wild and helpless look. "No, I don't think so. But naturally I'm shaken. I've made it clear that I'm not parent material—not anymore, anyway."

"Forty isn't ancient," she argued.

"But by this point, a man either has his life in order or he's searching for the missing pieces. I—"

"How can you think you have all the pieces together?" she cried out indignantly. "With no real ties of your own all these years. If you could only see what you've been missing!"

The slender hands trembling in her lap made his heart lurch. He'd gotten so much pleasure over the years out of being her knight, her hero. When she set her sights on a man, she meant business! "Look, honey, I know what being a father means. Hell, I have one! It takes dedication, a commitment to be there, a capacity to provide sound wisdom. I've always figured if I couldn't do the job right, I had no right to do the job."

Jane popped up from the cushions, her raven hair and peach hem swirling. "What a fool I was to believe that you'd come around and graciously accept your responsibilities. You are far too self-centered—"

"The word is *involved*," he protested.

She waved dismissively. "No matter. Call it involved, absorbed, or whatever, self is the bottom line with you always!"

Real pain darkened his strong features. "That's not true! You know I care for you, Jane."

"Not enough. Not in the right way!"

"Of course I'll stand by you," he hastened to assure.

"Don't knock yourself out."

He balked at her change of attitude. "Your behavior has always been so unpredictable. No matter what I say or how I say it, I'm in the wrong!"

"How do you expect me to behave? I'm a pregnant bride whose husband bristles with inconvenience at the news, walks around gingerly, as though he's wearing a noose around his neck."

"You make me sound like a horse's ass."

"Well, giddyap, pardner!"

He raked a hand through his fair hair. "I thought we were doing so well here these past weeks."

"It's been nice, to a point," she allowed. "Real nice. I'm sorry I spoiled the fun with my news." She tried to brush past him and down the hallway to the bedroom they shared, but he made a lunge to snag her arm. "Let me go!" She tried to jerk out of his reach, causing the amber liquid in his glass to slosh over the sides.

"We have to talk." He hauled her over to his rocker recliner, set down the glass with a thump and pulled her down with him into the deep chair. "This kind of stress can't be good for you."

"As if you care!" She squirmed in his lap, trying to get away.

But his voice was another matter. It was in soft, soothing counterpoint to his iron clasp. "We're just going to settle down together. Rocking, relaxing..."

"No!"

Greg cupped her tear-stained cheek in his huge palm and gently pushed her head down against the solid plane of his chest.

She was prepared to fight, accuse him all over again of being way too jaded for his own good, when she picked up the rapid beat of his heart beneath her cheek. He was frightened. Maybe as frightened as she. On that assumption, she decided to give him a chance.

Greg reached up to stroke her wavy mane of hair with shaky fingers as she burrowed into the soft folds of his blue terry shirt. Wildcat to kitten. Thank God! But didn't she always give in, because she loved him so much? Could he possibly deserve the works after all his years of rambling and carousing, doing as he damn well pleased?

Why wouldn't she listen? He'd tried to explain that he had limitations—had said so all along. But she consistently believed him capable of moving mountains, tracking down natives with rings. Though the ring reference in the letter to Sir had most likely been slanted to Mabel's way of thinking, the spirit of the whole thing reflected Jane's attitude, too. The Haleys had always considered the Baron men larger than life. It was so unrealistic.

Not that he hadn't been happy during their first month together.

Playing the devoted husband had proved quite satisfying. The future was not discussed. Each day was tackled for itself. They were a team, making love, keeping house, brainstorming over the management of the store. Her progress in the basement amazed and delighted him. Her verve would be so good for Sir and the store long after he was out of the management picture. If anybody could persuade Sir to move with the times, it was Janey. Clark Baron had actually seemed receptive to the changes she'd made in the basement. Jane had accomplished the impossible!

Greg had relished their day-to-day existence. But just as he was settling in, the stakes had taken this perilous jump. They were having a baby! He'd planted his seed and he was going to be a father!

They rocked on in a dozing state, each lost in their own private thoughts. Jane eventually reached a point where she could no longer stand the silence, the unknown.

"Greg?"

He opened his eyes as she was lifting her head from his chest. "Yeah?"

"It's never been my intention to trap you against your will. You know that, don't you?"

His strong features softened as he nodded.

She traced the length of his jaw with a slender finger, swallowing to keep her throat open. "If you don't think you can cut this, I want you to tell me now. Tonight. We will of course see the birth through together, for the baby's sake as much as anyone else's, but I have to know if you're willing to work toward a real future."

Greg shuddered nervously. Janey sure had a talent for cutting to the chase, for forcing him to face issues. "I've never felt as fulfilled as I have with you these past few weeks," he rasped, desperately trying to piece together an honest, but gentle response. "But I am who I am. I love my career of choice. The idea of drawing a clean slate isn't feasible. I can't throw Explore Unlimited away to slip into Dad's shoes." He sighed, pressing his lips to her temple. "So you see, a whole lot depends on what you expect from me as a father and a husband."

How clever of him to toss the ball back into her court, she thought with a wince. "Look, I confess that I was counting on you settling in at the Emporium," she confided in a small voice. "But that wasn't fair of me. I've really enjoyed our marriage, and I do want to keep working at it."

He lifted his brows in wonder. She wasn't going to argue with him. Wasn't going to try to reshape his goals. How did she manage to always pull the unexpected on him? Excite him? Challenge him to be his best?

"How the hell do you make it so easy to love you, honey?"

She sighed softly, nuzzling his neck. "If you think I'm easy to love, just wait until you hold our baby for the first time."

Greg rubbed the length of her back, releasing a small silent sigh of his own. Thank God she hadn't had the brass to question his love for the baby they were making together. Despite their conflicts, his doubts about his own capabilities, he already had feelings for the child.

"Honey," he began on a tentative note. "I am going to have to make a trip to Los Angeles next week."

She gave his chest a gentle pound. "Rats."

"You knew my leaving was inevitable," he chided with a tweak to her nose. "Faxes and telephone calls can only accomplish so much. Nicole's rounded up some possible hosts for our English village tour, and all sorts—"

"Let Grimes do the hosting."

"He's a Texan!" he scoffed.

Her eyes danced. "But he's as cool and capable as any Limey could be."

"I'm looking for someone with real knowledge of the country, a native. And we need to set things up soon, if we're going to shoot in autumn."

"Well, you can't blame a girl for trying, can you?"

"Nope. But you can envision all the work waiting for me."

Her expression grew more earnest. "Yeah, I understand. It's the way I feel about the Emporium. Loose ends. Endless possibilities."

"Well, you'll certainly have enough to keep you occupied during my absence, with work, and now planning for the baby. I imagine it was quite a shock to you, too," he realized tardily.

"Oh, yeah." She pushed out her lower lip under his solicitous gaze. "Guess this is my first test on flexibility, huh?"

"Yup. But I think you'll agree that we're on very steady ground together right now, Janey. Our relationship has grown. We'll fit the child into what we have."

He slipped a hand under the skirt of her dress to rub her belly. She gasped as his fingers traced over the elastic ridge of her panties.

"You know, I have noticed a little weight gain on you lately," he said, continuing his intimate exploration. "Thought it was too much of your own good cooking."

"Oh, you!" she shrieked.

"Let's go to bed." With a lurching motion, Greg rose from the chair with Jane scooped up against his chest.

As they started down the hallway, the blinking light on his fax machine from his small study caught his eye. He paused for a second, then began to move on toward the bedroom.

"Hey, aren't you going to get that?" she asked.

He arched a roguish brow. "It can't be more important than our bedtime."

"Oh, go ahead," she urged.

"Really?" he queried with open appreciation. "You don't mind the intrusion?"

"Flexible Mrs. Baron mind? Not on your life!"

Greg gently eased to her to her feet and moved into the study. "I'll only be a minute," he said, switching on the overhead light.

"That's all right," she lilted, sidling up behind him as he peeled the printed page free of the machine.

He read the message, then slowly turned, his eyes narrowed and silvered. "Janey..."

Her Cupid's-bow mouth twitched. "What, darling?"

"This fax is from my L.A. office."

"Aren't they all?" she chirped, peeking over his arm to read the message aloud. "'Congratulations on your new production.' That is really sweet, you know?"

His features grew wry. "But how did Kevin know to be sweet?"

She folded her arms across her chest. "Gee, you're suspicious."

"Janey!"

"Okay," she relented on a sigh. "It's just my way of fighting back. I had to do something to stake my claim."

"Honey, Nicole is not going to steal me away."

Jane drew a smug smile. "Not if it gets complicated enough, she won't!"

"Our relationship cannot get more complex than it is at this moment," he lamented.

She pressed her lips together to bite back a retort. He was a naive fool to believe the problems with Nicole would just evaporate. "Well, she'll be madder than hell about this and might not even speak to you," she forecast with glee.

"She's more mature than that." He tossed the sheet of paper on his desk and turned back to confront Jane. "Nicole fully understands that she can never reach me the way you have."

"So she has tried!"

"Yes. But can you blame her? We were man and wife at the time!"

She shook a finger at him. "There's a dodge if I ever heard one. She still wants you."

"Maybe, on some level," he finally admitted. "But it's not enough."

"I imagine at forty, she's ready to settle for whatever it is."

"Ha! Shows again how little you know about being forty!" She tried to turn away, but he spun her back. "You aren't leaving this room until I hammer a little logic into your noggin."

"Good luck!"

"You expect me to act like a carefree romantic at forty. You don't think I'm past it. So, therefore, you should believe that Nicole, too, has dreams of her own. She simply hasn't found anybody who is just right."

"Okay, okay. You win."

He stopped short in amazement. "I do?"

"Yes, you do."

His gaze sharpened. "Why?"

She threw her arms into the air. "Because if we keep this up, we'll never get to bed."

"So you want this old bag of bones down on the mat, do you?"

Her eyes held a lusty gleam. "Mmm-hmm..."

He raised his squared chin. "Maybe I'm not in the mood anymore."

"You don't have to worry about scrambling for birth control," she coaxed, stepping back with a provocative sway.

He stared off into space. "Well..."

She reached under her peach-colored dress and slipped off her panties. "Remember these?"

"Sort of..."

"Take a closer look." She tossed them into his face.

He peeled the scrap of cotton off his nose and crushed them with a mock growl. "You're gonna get it."

"I'm beginning to wonder!" she mocked. Flapping her skirt up to her face, she scurried out of the room.

"Hey, you haven't pulled that little trick for my attention since you were three!"

"Well, it got me a new tricycle back then," she called out.

He quietly crept down the hallway to the bedroom to discover her standing naked before the dresser mirror, brushing her shiny cascade of hair. Now that he knew of her condition, he could more clearly recognize the changes in her shape. Her breasts were enlarged and her belly was taking a rounder pear shape. He suddenly felt engulfed in a foreign state of ignorance.

Her nose wrinkled in the reflection as she spotted him. "Slowpoke," she purred in innuendo.

Greg glided up behind her and wedged his hardness into her bottom.

"Guess what, little mama?"

She leaned back into him. "What?"

"I'm all out of tricycles."

"GREG, ARE YOU LISTENING to me?" Kevin prodded.

Greg recrossed the feet he had propped on the desk and regarded his partner with a blank expression. "Huh?"

"You fly in here for one of your marathon work sessions, then you fall into a trance."

Greg grinned, tapping the open book in his lap. "Some very interesting sketches of the female form in here."

"No kidding?" With a roguish look, the dark stocky director rounded Greg's chair for a peek.

"See?" Greg said, slowly flipping through the pages. "One for every month."

But it wasn't the string of enticing calendar girls Kevin had anticipated, but sideview drawings of a woman with child, depicting the development stages of the fetus in the womb. *"The Miracle of Pregnancy?"*

"Yeah. I want to understand everything that's happening to Jane."

"Good idea, I suppose." Kevin's disappointment swiftly evolved into curiosity as Greg tracked the characteristics a baby possessed by the second trimester. "The kid already has a heartbeat at four months? Naw . . ."

Greg nodded, his expression just as awestruck. "One that can be heard with a stethoscope. And he sucks his thumb, too. My baby will be there pretty soon," he added proudly. "At six weeks, his heart is already developing, as are his nervous system and lungs."

Kevin sank into his own chair across the aisle. "This is all new territory to us." He snapped his fingers suddenly, as he often did when inspiration struck him. "Had we known about this pregnancy earlier, we could've planned an instructional video for expectant fathers."

Greg grinned, closing the book, tossing it on the desk. "I thought of that myself yesterday during the plane ride."

"Jane would be perfect for it," Kevin decided with a sure nod of his head. "Well, maybe we can catch her in time, next time."

Greg nearly toppled out of his spring-loaded chair. "Huh?"

"It isn't as mercenary as it sounds," Kevin assured with a wave of a pencil. "You'll no doubt plan the second child. We'll start the preproduction process, before you start the baby production. Whaddaya say?"

Greg gulped. "I haven't quite come to terms with this first one."

"Hell, one's not enough. Who's the kid going to play with?"

"My father," Greg replied grandly.

Kevin was still chuckling when Nicole breezed through the office door moments later.

"Oh. I miss something . . . more?"

"No," Greg promptly replied. "You're up to speed on the wedding and the pregnancy. There really isn't much more I can do, is there?"

Her eyes snapped. "No."

Greg took the time to appraise her from head to toe. Her cropped blond hair had some new wave to it, her face held traces of makeup, and her outfit—a red dress and black leggings—was far more dramatic than the usual crisp cotton khaki.

She instinctively folded her arms across her chest. "You got a problem, Baron?"

"No, Nik, I'm just a little intrigued by the transformation."

"Well, it's not for you," she returned sharply. "I just hope to make Stephen Humphries comfortable during our conference."

"Ah, so you did manage to snag him!" Greg rejoiced. "Great!" The British author-humorist had been his first choice for host all along. He was famous on both sides of the ocean for his keen wit and easy style. "Can I assume that you intend to reel him in this morning from the airport?"

"If you mean, am I going to go pick him up in the company Cadillac, yes!"

"We've scraped up a few other possibilities," Kevin put in, fully aware that his words would be falling on deaf ears. "Just in case we can't come to terms with good old Stephen."

"No need!" Greg and Nicole chorused in alarm.

"I'm sure your intentions with this eligible bachelor are honorable," Greg teased.

"Well, you can't blame me for being a little starstuck," Nicole fumed with hands on hips. "But don't think you can tease your way out of what you've done. You went ahead and remarried, Greg, without even consulting me."

Greg tipped back in his chair, regarding her through hooded lids. He could explain how sudden it was, how temporary and necessary it had seemed that night, but he refused to do it. It would only give Nicole a glimmer of hope that they could continue on at some level of intimacy.

Once and for all, he wanted to put a stop to all of it.

"I truly believe, Nik, that your anger centers more around Jane having me, than on you not having me."

"Well, it's a little of both," she ground out bluntly. "Boy, do I wish I'd been on hand at the ceremony. I'd have rushed down the aisle and jumped into your arms. Doomed her union the way she doomed mine!"

"What a sight that would'a been," Kevin gibed. "Somebody would've called 911 for sure."

"Shut up!"

Greg suppressed a smirk as he, too, visualized the scene. "Nik, Jane was only five when she did that to you!"

"Already a miniature manipulator."

Greg rubbed his temples. "Cripes, woman."

She suddenly noted the book he'd tossed on the desk, bringing to issue their second milestone. "And what timing she has! Manages to conceive your child before the wedding ring's halfway over her knuckle. You didn't want a child with me!"

"We were students. Just starting out!" His voice grew stern as he drilled her with his steely eyes and a dose of the facts. "You didn't want a child, either."

"But now I wish we'd—" She broke off helplessly. "He'd be in college now. Preparing to take over that department store of your father's."

"You never liked my father and thought the store was a dump!"

"But—"

"You're upset that I've settled down first," he stated firmly, keeping a tight rein on his temper. "You can do the same. If you make an effort."

"Well, I guess I'll go ahead out to the airport," she said tersely, grabbing the Caddy's keys from his desk, nearly severing his fingers in the drawer.

"She could turn her love life around if she really wanted to," Kevin groused, once the door shut on her again.

Greg's mouth compressed in a grim line. "I partly blame myself. We never should've kept up our relationship—in business or in bed. She would've tried harder to begin again if she hadn't had me to lean on."

"She's way over the age of consent," Kevin retorted. "Don't let her wreck this new life you have. If she believes she has an inch of clearance, she'll wedge her way in there. Face it!"

Greg rubbed his temples with a nod. "I will. Jane and I already are faced with so many challenges. I can't let Nicole become one of them."

9

"ALL THIS SUBTERFUGE has me in a whirl, Janey," Mabel professed the following Saturday at the Baron condo.

Jane drew a wry smile across the cluttered spare bedroom. They were fixing it up for the baby and it was a literal construction zone, with plastic covering the slate-gray carpet, sizing spread on the walls, and all the equipment needed for hanging wallpaper, including a creaky old wooden stepladder. Mabel was dressed like an aging artist in a faded aqua smock and old white polyester pants, her white curls crushed beneath a bandanna. Jane was in one of Greg's cast-off dress shirts and her largest elastic shorts, her long mane captured in a barrette. Nothing much fit her properly anymore. And certainly not the tight cutoffs and T-shirts she generally wore for projects like this one.

"I think Greg will be delighted with this surprise," Jane objected patiently under her grandma's distressed look. "He'll be proud that I didn't waste away my time worrying about how he was handling Nicole. Don't you see? It's my way of proving that we can work everything out."

"I'm not talking about the room," Mabel protested. "It's the due dates."

"Now, Grandma," Jane chided. "Fretting about the dates will only make your confusion grow. It's as easy as one, two, three."

"Not more numbers, Janey! Please!"

Jane picked up a double roll of the wallpaper and began to unwind it on their long fold-out worktable. She paused to smile at the teddy-bear figures picknicking on the washable vinyl. "Well, dear, we wouldn't have to pretend today at all if you hadn't invited Sir over to help us out."

Mabel placed her hand on her hip with a huff. "I would have much rather spent this time alone with you. But he was ranting on about sending in a decorator to do up the room. He wanted to upstage me, pure and simple, and I wouldn't hear of it."

"They do like their services," Jane concurred with new understanding.

"Well, we want our baby to learn the joys of self-sufficiency," Mabel proclaimed heartily. "I loved Amanda to pieces, God bless her soul, but she missed so much in her sheltered world."

"There's a class division between our families—where such things as services are concerned," Jane agreed fretfully. "I hope it won't be a problem. I expect the baby to be a bit of a do-it-yourselfer as we are."

"A monied person can be handy," Mabel assured.

Jane recalled what Greg had said about Sir endowing Mabel and smiled. Her grandmother certainly practiced what she preached. She could coast through her seventies if she wanted to, but she was always on the go, with her housework, her crafts, her charities. Why, Mabel delivered meals to folks not much older than herself!

"Sir will just have to come to accept that the Haleys don't care to be catered to," Jane decided, her mind on the Emporium as well as the nursery. Sir had reluctantly accepted the fact that she was staying in the Bargain Basement. Encouraged, Jane was anxious to push him another step forward, to begin further innovations throughout the store. There was so much to face and so little time to face it. The baby would be here in a matter of months, and the store would crash and burn soon thereafter if something drastic wasn't done.

"Let's go over the scam once again," Mabel asked.

Jane was aghast. "It isn't a scam!"

"Forgive the poor choice of terms, dear," Mabel impatiently apologized. "But time is running out."

"Okay. Sir has the real due date in November. He knew I was pregnant even before I did."

"How clever of Clark," Mabel twittered with twinkling eyes.

Jane gritted her teeth. "It's because you told him in the letter, Grandma. Before you told me, remember?"

"How clever of me," she happily amended.

Jane shook her head, measuring the wallpaper with a T square. "Yeah, sure."

"Well, it got you two married, didn't it?"

She eyed Mabel dolefully. "Yes, Grandma, it did. And if you want us to stay married, you have to keep all of this straight for Greg, as well."

"What's his angle again?"

Jane paused, grinding on her bubble gum. "Okay. Greg thinks I conceived on our wedding night, so he believes the baby is due late December, early January. That's when everyone at the store thinks the baby's coming, too."

Mabel furrowed her brow as she absorbed the information. "It would've been simpler to have told him the truth right away."

"I wish I had!" she lamented. "We've grown so close. I know him so much better. I realize now that I could have trusted him to understand. But it was a spur-of-the-moment decision right before the wedding. I had shut him down so thoroughly." She sighed bleakly. "Oh, Gran, I was afraid he'd storm out of my life for good. And that wouldn't have been fair to the baby!"

Mabel clucked in sympathy, bustling past the stepladder and worktable to pull the pear-shaped Jane close.

"I don't like to promote this confusion, but I'm in so deep now. I can only hope Greg believes that the baby is early."

Mabel released her, looking down at Jane's growing paunch. "That's bound to be the biggest premmie on record, my girl."

Jane inhaled sharply. "I was a small baby, you said so."

She lifted a finger in protest. "Ah, but Gregory was a chunk. A ten pounder."

"Ouch!"

Mabel winced with a nod.

"Well, we'll just have to pray for a later delivery and downsized child."

"I imagine I can do that without fretting over the numbers game," Mabel complied.

The chime of the doorbell interrupted. "That must be Clark," Jane wagered, swiping her moist eyes with the back of her hand. She moved through the condo, and swung open the door. The twelfth-floor hallway looked a zoo. Stuffed animals in a variety of colors and sizes were crowded around the door.

Jane clasped her hands in delight. "More guests for the teddy bears' picnic!"

Clark's silver head popped up behind a giant giraffe. "Surely you didn't expect the proud grandpapa to come empty-handed, did you?"

Jane took one of the larger brown furry bears out of his path. "Come in, please."

Clark hauled the giraffe inside along with him. Grimes appeared in the doorway, proceeding to transfer all the other stuffed creatures into the living room. Both men were dressed in casual twill slacks and light cotton shirts appropriate for work.

"How thoughtful of you!" Jane murmured, kissing Sir's rigid jawline.

"I could've had the whole room done up for you," he declared, his mouth set in grumpy confusion. "Saved you all this trouble."

"Now, Clark," Mabel schooled from the hallway. "Didn't I explain nesting to you just the other day?"

"You did, Mabel," he admitted. "And I've decided it might be a good tonic, even for me."

"Dr. Crane made the decision concerning the decorating project," Grimes amended with a pleasant smile. "He thought that perhaps the pasting of the wallpaper might be just the job for Sir. He did, however, advise you not to allow him to measure or align it on the walls."

"Oh, shut your trap," Clark snapped in embarrassment.

"It's for your own good, Sir, not to get too riled. The hedge-clipping was a complete failure," Grimes informed the women. "We have to replace some of the shrubbery and Sir's blood pressure soared."

"Well, we have that in common," Jane intimated, linking her arm in Sir's. "My pressure has been a little too high, as well."

Clark's brows instantly jumped toward his hairline. "You should be in bed!"

Jane laughed gently, guiding him in the direction of the bedrooms. "No, no, it's just a matter of getting a proper amount of rest, and avoiding undue stress."

Clark's eyes widened in horror as they all entered the shambles of the nursery.

"Jane perceives this sort of project as fun," Grimes cautioned his employer.

"Relaxing fun," Jane concurred, as she moved over to the worktable. "I was just cutting my first piece of wallpaper. You like it?"

"Yes, yes, of course," Clark assured, stepping closer.

"Your job will be easy," Jane told him as she reached for a pencil and knife. "This paper is prepasted, so all you'll have to do is dip it in that molded plastic trough at the end of the table, water it down."

"That was to be my job," Mabel protested with a childish pout.

Jane shot her an incredulous look. "Grandma!"

"I had it all set in my mind how it's done," she declared huffily. "You made me practice. Now you pass it over to Clark! Why, this whole deal is due to my let—"

"Okay," Jane interrupted, fearful that Mabel would spill too much in her tirade. "It's true, Sir. Grandma has been practicing. How would you like to take the paper from her, fold it, and bring it to me at the ladder?"

"You're going to climb that rickety old ladder?" Clark roared with a shake of a gnarled finger.

Jane balked for an answer. When one didn't spring to mind, she burst into tears.

"Now see what you've done!" Grimes chastised the elderly pair, winding an arm around the sobbing Jane.

"We're only trying to help," Mabel insisted. "Aren't we, Clark?"

"Of course we are!" he bellowed, his face pinched in concern.

"You two are just angling to be most important," Grimes surmised sternly. "It's brought out the competitive spirit in you."

"Well, I am the great-grandmother," Mabel declared. "But no matter, there's room for everyone to have a share in the joy."

Joy? In-laws at odds is joy? Jane cupped her hands to her face with a wail.

"I don't understand it," Clark complained with fear in his eyes. "She was smiling a moment ago. Atop the world with this silly project!"

Jane glared through her fingers. "It's not silly to be handy!"

"Of course it isn't," Grimes concurred, giving her shoulders a squeeze. "These mood swings are perfectly natural to an expectant mother, Sir," he went on to explain to his employer.

"I can't remember these things," Clark erupted defensively. "It's been forty years since Amanda carried Greg."

"Oh, how I wish Greg were here," Jane confided tearfully.

"There's one wish I understand and can grant," Sir ground out with a curled fist. "I'll just call that son of mine and tell him—"

"No!" Jane squealed, causing them all to regard her in surprise. "No," she repeated more firmly with a sniff. "He feels trapped enough, as it is. If he wants to share in these kinds of things, he has to do it of his own free will."

Mabel moved up beside Clark, setting a freckled hand on his arm. "She has the right idea, I believe. We got them married and that's all we can do. Aside from our wallpapering tasks. I will wet the paper and you will fold it. Agreed?"

Sir bobbed his gray head with a milder expression. "Agreed."

"I will do my part by holding the ladder steady," Grimes announced in marked warning to Sir.

"As long as she's not dizzy," Clark returned, with a frown of concern at Jane.

Jane blinked, her blue eyes brightening. "No, I'm feeling fine. Really."

They worked diligently through the afternoon. By early evening the nursery was papered and most of the mess was cleared away.

"I believe I need a breath of fresh air," Jane declared as they eyed their handiwork. "How about some iced tea on the balcony? I have a fresh pitcher in the fridge."

"Grand idea!" Sir enthused. "A bit of a celebration for a job well done."

"I'll tend to the last of this cleanup," Grimes offered, folding the ladder in two.

"Yes, you and Clark go on ahead," Mabel prompted, adjusting the scarf on her head as she gathered up the brushes and tools. "I'll just continue on here with Grimes."

"Come along, little mother," Clark urged with a firm hand on Jane's elbow. "You can humor *me* for a while!"

Jane allowed her father-in-law to pamper her, making her comfortable in a lounger out on the wrought-iron balcony overlooking Kellogg Boulevard. City traffic was brisk on the streets twelve stories below, due to the lure of St. Paul's trendy restaurants and active artistic community.

"I sometimes miss the hustle and bustle down here on the weekends," Clark confided, arranging her tall glass of tea and a plate of cookies on a small table at her side.

"And I often long for your spacious backyard," she returned with a smile.

"We'll have to make sure the baby has plenty of space to play," he remarked, sinking into the chair at the foot of her lounger.

"We will," she replied, sipping on her drink. "There's plenty of time for that sort of planning. The nursery is a dandy start. The baby will spend much of its early time in there."

"You'll need a nice rocking chair, a dresser, a lamp. All sorts of things," he decided excitedly.

Jane giggled as she absorbed a cookie in two bites.

Clark's weathered face crinkled. "I love to hear that sound, Janey. Your laughter is like a tonic to me. Always has been."

"Thank you," she said tenderly, reaching forward to give his extended hand a squeeze. "For being the man in my life all these years."

He flushed with pleasure, kissing her fingers before settling back in his chair. "I know I've always played second fiddle to my own son, but that's the way it should be. This is the happy ending I've always hoped for. You and Gregory, settling down together. Linking our families with a child. If only he would settle down completely, take over for me." His expression crumpled somewhat.

"Greg and I have been very happy together," she assured around a second cookie. "But I believe he's only so flexible, only willing to compromise up to a certain point. He loves his career and we have no right to force him to give it all up."

"But the Emporium is the Baron lifeline," he asserted.

"That's something I've been thinking long and hard about," she ventured to admit.

"You? How?"

Jane sought to suppress her irritation over his doubtful surprise. "Sir, I know you're set in your ways about a wife's role in the home."

Clark stared down into his tea thoughtfully. "It's the tried-and-true way."

She smiled patiently. "Now, didn't Amanda help you out in the store?"

"Sometimes," he admitted slowly. "But it never interfered with her household duties."

"Well, it just goes to show you that a woman can budget her time," she bantered. "I can only imagine the hours she spent planning business dinners and cocktail parties for you, too."

"I admit that we were partners."

She could sense he was wavering. "Just look at the good I've done in the Bargain Basement since Greg transferred me down there."

"Yes, yes," he reluctantly admitted. "I've been watching the figures. They are soaring under your direction."

She inhaled, deciding the time would never be better to launch into her campaign for recognition. "It's my opinion that visual techniques are at the bottom of good selling. They're what got me bounced out of Toys in the first place, but it was a successful campaign."

"Really?" he questioned with interest. "I was so enamored with the news of the baby, that I never did delve into what went wrong with Nibling."

"Well, Greg probably thought it best to soft-peddle the issues at the time, but I think you're strong enough to deal with it now, don't you?"

His narrow chest puffed a bit under his work shirt. "Certainly."

Jane detailed her Plas-Tek demonstration and the surge in sales. She bit her tongue about the lost commissions. Instead, she focused on Nibling's tunnel vision and inability to open himself to proven methods.

Clark listened intently, clasping his hands together, pressing his lips to a thin line. "So what would you like me to do, Jane? Fire Nibs?"

"No, this isn't a personal vendetta," she hastily assured. "No, what I have in mind encompasses all the managers. I'd like to take a survey, find out what they honestly think of their departments, how they'd like to improve them."

"Don't they already have the option of voicing their opinions?"

Jane reached for another cookie with a tsk.

"Maybe you should have some dinner before you spoil your appetite," he suggested.

"Oh, I'm hungry all the time," she said in blithe dismissal.

"So, what about these managers?" he pressed. "I thought everybody was happy."

"Now, Sir," she chided between nibbles. "You know you aren't very approachable on the subject of change."

"Why, I . . ." He stumbled over his words. "I've done a fair job with the store over the years. Hell, I've made a fortune!"

"Of course you have! It's just that times are changing rapidly."

"I don't want to run a quick-stop market," he retorted, obviously having used this excuse before. "Like that self-service in the suburbs. The Baron name stands for quality and dignity."

"And that can be part of the hook," she persisted with mounting excitement.

"I don't understand."

"Well, how would it be to combine the best of Baron's with the best of the modernized merchandising? Keep the service, but make the departments more airy, more accessible." Her hands were animated as she reached for another cookie. "We could increase the lighting, widen the aisles, take the less expensive items out of the glass cases, find out what is selling and what is not. Oh, Sir, it could be so wonderful!"

Clark Baron stared into her shining eyes for a long pensive moment. "You love the store as I do, don't you? I . . . never realized that. Not totally."

"Only because I'm a woman," she said with gentle firmness.

"A woman with a baby to raise," he swiftly returned.

She had to smile at his earnest look. "Look, I think I can do it all. I want the chance to prove it."

He stroked his jaw. "I don't know, dear. I just don't know."

"What harm can it do if I put some of my theories into motion before the baby arrives?" she wheedled.

His eyes drilled her. "What of your high blood pressure?"

"I believe our blood pressure will drop if we meet a challenge we both love."

It was Sir's turn to laugh. "Ah, perhaps. I will admit that I know there are problems with our profit margin."

"Greg did his best to right the Emporium's course." Jane couldn't help reminding.

"Yes, he did. And I imagine you think I'm a soft touch right now because of your condition." He leaned forward in his chair. "But let me tell you this. As elated as I am about your new status in the family, it's your love of the Emporium that makes me listen to you. I brushed Greg and his recommendations off because he didn't care enough, because the store is a pain to him. It bruised my heart and my ego that he hoped to breeze into my world, fix it up, and fly off again." He shook a finger at her. "But you, Janey, you have the sort of interest that I admire."

She licked the traces of sugar from her mouth with an anxious look. "So, shall we give my way a try?"

"Yes, let's do it." He reached over and took away the plate of cookies before she could snatch another one. "Let's go into the house and have some real food to celebrate."

"Great idea!" she rejoiced, sliding off the lounger. "I have a roast, and some rice and some beans and some pie. It'll be wonderful!"

Just as they did with the nursery, the foursome pitched in to prepare the meal. Jane ate more than the tall, sturdy Grimes, but no one had the grace or courage to comment. They were just settling back with coffee in the living room when the telephone rang. Grimes immediately answered the cordless with the same salutation he used at the estate.

"Grimey?" Greg demanded at the other end of the line, openly shocked to hear the servant's voice.

"Yes, Gregory. No, you haven't made a mistake." He fleetingly covered the mouthpiece to filter out Sir's snort. "We're dining with Jane and her grandmother this evening. Of course. One moment." Grimes circled the coffee table and crossed the sitting area to present Jane with the telephone.

She snatched it with a grin and a nod. "Hello, Greg?"

"Are you all right?"

Jane beamed at her guests. "Yes, I'm wonderful."

"I was hoping you'd be alone."

Her thin black brows furrowed as she broke eye contact with Sir. "Why, darling?"

"Well, because I have some bad news."

"What?" she asked with forced cheer. She was determined to absorb the news, decide how bad it was before passing it on.

"We've gotten a tentative yes from Humphries. He's going to host our show."

"That's good news isn't it?"

"What's he saying?" Sir interrupted sharply, preparing to pounce out of his chair.

"Greg's lined up a host for his tour of Britain," she paused to report.

Clark sank back in his chair. "Yippee."

Jane turned her attention back to the phone. "Your father sends his congratulations, darling."

"I heard."

"So, is there anything else?"

"Baby, I . . . I have to take a trip over to England."

"When?"

"Now."

"But you were supposed to come home tomorrow night!" she sputtered indignantly, abandoning the idea of concealing his news from the family.

"I know, but Humphries isn't entirely satisfied with a couple of the villages I've chosen to spotlight. He'd like to show me better ones."

"Damn him, this guy! You're already planning to spend part of September and all of October over there!"

"Now, honey, I think your condition is speaking for you."

"Just what do you know of my condition?"

"Well, I bought a book on pregnancy—"

"You bought a book!" she shrieked.

"And I read that—"

"You bought one lousy book and you read it and suddenly you're an expert? Well, damn you, too!"

"Jane, Humphries won't do the deal unless I compromise, listen to his point of view—"

"That's what marriage is supposed to be about—compromise, point of view!"

"Janey, don't let this setback upset you so."

"Is Nicole going along?"

"No."

As angry as she was, Jane couldn't help but release a sigh of relief. "How long will you be gone?"

"I don't think I'd better tell you now."

"Tell me now or I'll hop on a plane for L.A. tonight."

"Okay, three weeks or so."

"Greg!"

"Janey, what happened to my understanding wife?"

"Ohh!"

Clark was on his feet. "Let me speak to him."

"Keep my father out of this, Jane."

She sighed hard, keeping her hand clamped to the instrument under Sir's demanding glare. "There's something we can agree on."

"Once you simmer down, I hope you'll try to understand."

"Maybe. If I wasn't pregnant. If every week didn't count for something."

"I know, honey. I love you. But I'm trapped. Several million dollars are at stake. Money that doesn't belong to me. You wouldn't want me to renege."

Her features and voice fell. "No, I know you have obligations."

"We're leaving first thing in the morning. I'll call you when we arrive."

"All right."

"This isn't a good time for us to talk, not with all of those invasive ears on your end."

Her eyes moistened. "I know. Have a safe trip." Before Sir could get ahold of the telephone, she pushed the disconnect button.

"So what is going on?" Mabel asked.

"Greg has to travel to Europe to scout some new locations," Jane reported quietly. "He'll be away for about three weeks."

"That's preposterous!" Clark roared. "You should've let me speak to him!"

"No, you would've fought and made matters worse," she retorted in all honesty. "It's better to just let him go."

"Well, you have all of us," Grimes soothed, with a nod of his silvered head.

"And you've got to get busy in our store," Clark went on with forced cheer. "Starting Monday morning, I've got myself a new assistant!"

Jane gazed up at him through moistened eyes. She would throw herself into her work for the time being, just as Greg was doing. But it was bound to be only a temporary diversion, the sort that often worked well in a childless marriage. Could Greg ever warm up to his family enough to satisfy her? Would he even try?

10

GREG ARRIVED HOME on the last Wednesday in May. He went directly from the airport to the Emporium. Judging from his phone calls to Jane over the past few weeks, he presumed she was ensconced in the seventh-floor offices with Sir, slipping into the apprenticeship role that had never quite suited him. Envy niggled in the corner of his mind over their harmonious arrangement, but it was the price he would have to pay to see his father satisfied and Baron's alive once again. More than anything he was glad that Sir was almost his old self physically and emotionally. If Greg himself couldn't step into Sir's shoes, his wife was the next best thing. It all could work out. They all could be happy together.

Because of Jane's helping hand with Sir and the store, Greg had found he could relax and enjoy his trip abroad, tromping from one English village to another, scouting sites with the dashing Humphries. The Brit was only a few years older than Greg, and quite likable. They'd gotten to know each other rather well. Humphries, like Greg, had spent most of his adult life single. As luck would have it, he was taken with Nicole. Naturally Nik had wanted to accompany them on the trip and Humphries would have preferred it. But at the time Greg hadn't known a romantic seed had been planted between the two of them. Nor could he have put Jane through the torture of wondering what Nicole was doing with him in England.

He couldn't wait to tell her that Nicole would have a shot at a fresh start! It would make his future commutes to the Los

Angeles office, as well as the production trip to London this fall, far more comfortable.

Greg breezed into his father's suite, greeting Sir's secretary and the two male assistants working in the outer office. He was relieved to find Clark Baron seated behind his desk, looking robust and in control as he rifled through his mail.

"Afternoon, Dad!"

Sir's bushy brows shot up and his mouth curved in welcome. "Well, well, the prodigal son returns. Or shall I say the prodigal father..."

Greg unbuttoned his jacket and eased into a chair on the opposite side of Sir's massive old cherrywood desk. "How's Jane? Where is Jane?" he asked in afterthought, looking around the room for any sign of his wife's things. He did spot a feminine powder-blue sweater hanging in the open closet.

"Jane is down in the Bargain Basement," Sir replied, setting aside his letter opener to focus exclusively on his son.

Greg drew a perplexed frown. "But why?"

Sir chuckled warmly. "Oh, it's sort of her other baby, I guess. She wants to make it the best it can be."

Greg stroked his rigid jaw. How ironic that it was her banishment to the basement that had started all the commotion in the first place. Now, even when she could be up in the executive suite all day long if she wished, she was planted down there!

"Something wrong with that?" Sir snapped in the lapse of silence.

"No, no, of course not," he assured with a wave. "Whatever the arrangement, you're obviously thriving with it."

"We both have managed to lower our blood pressure," he reported proudly.

"Both?" Greg's pulse hammered in his ears. Jane was having trouble and hadn't said a thing!

Clark sized up the situation with a keen look. "I believe that you were trapped into this trip. But I suggest you carefully arrange your future dealings. You've missed a lot this month. For instance, I've been playing coach at her childbirth classes Friday noons over at the YWCA. We've been to three out of four."

"Well, I'll be at the final one," Greg vowed, struggling to keep his tone level. Why had she gone ahead and jumped into those classes so quickly? Out of spite?

His father was watching him keenly, hoping for a chance to hash over Greg's personal business. Greg wished only to terminate the surprising and painful avenue of discussion. It killed him to think that his own father was privy to intimate knowledge about his wife before he was, sharing moments that were rightfully his. But he knew the old man was so excited about the child that he would insinuate himself wherever there was an opening. It was up to Greg to throttle him back. To assert his position as head of his own home.

"Well, I'm happy to hear the store is on the upswing," he went on to say with a shift to the only other subject of keen interest to Sir. "I got the impression from Jane's calls and letters that she's in the thick of things."

"Oh, she is," Sir concurred heartily. "But we've only begun. I insisted upon starting slow, using the basement as sort of a prototype department, a place to experiment with new and innovative techniques. Well, damned if she isn't pulling out all the stops to prove her points! Sales in the basement are on the steady incline." He lifted his shoulders a fraction. "Some things have worked, others haven't. We're getting all the bugs out."

Greg raked his long fingers through his sun-bleached hair, struggling with another painful jab. "You mean like widening the aisles, making merchandise more accessible, adding more light, more registers—"

"Yes, and hiring on younger, more informed buyers," he finished evenly. "I know it sounds like an echo to you, boy."

"I'm happy for you, Dad, of course," he hastened to assure, studying his blunt fingernails. "But it is a little disheartening to learn that you couldn't take those same ideas from me some months ago."

Clark drew a wistful smile. "I know you love me, Gregory. We've always had the sort of relationship where love could be openly expressed. But it has always rankled me that you never took to the store. Now Janey, she really loves this business. She isn't just lighting here out of duty, to meet family obligations." He pounded on the desktop with a veined fist. "Her heart and soul are part of the deal."

"I'm sorry I couldn't deliver that!"

"Don't get hot about it, boy. Not now, when everything has balanced so well. Naturally, I will always be a little disappointed that you refused to make a go of the Emporium, but you've come through with the happily-forever solution that really works for everyone."

"In other words I had the wisdom to marry well," he translated on a wry note.

Clark's gray eyes twinkled. "As you say. But please don't feel unappreciated, Gregory. I recognize your sacrifice to stay on here since my attack, your struggle to represent me even when you didn't agree with my policies. Jane explained about her clash with Nibling, your patience with him, when you'd much rather have socked him in the nose!"

"I did try to tell you all about that," Greg couldn't resist adding in reminder.

"Hell, boy, I know it. But the only thing I could see in Jane's letter was that baby." His face beamed like a light bulb. "My precious grandchild."

"Am I correct in assuming that I'm no longer needed around the store?" Greg asked mildly.

"To the contrary!" Sir instantly retorted. "I'm going to need all the help I can get during our upcoming transition period. And I was hoping to take Mabel on the trip up to Brainerd this week—starting tomorrow, now that you're back. I plan to tour the resorts, wine and dine her a bit. Nothing romantic, of course. Grimes will be coming along."

"Just three old friends taking some leisure time," Greg surmised with understanding and approval. "It sounds like a wonderful idea."

"I know you haven't had a honeymoon, yet," Sir murmured sympathetically. "But I figure that you'll do something nice after the baby's born and Jane is feeling fit again."

"My plan exactly." Greg rose to his feet. "Well, I believe I'll just take a trip to the bottom, drop in on my little entrepreneur."

"By all means," Clark encouraged, retrieving his letter opener. "She's running some big sales spectacle this week. I don't know much about it. Promised to butt out."

"You? Butt out?" Greg pulled a good-natured grin. "She isn't an entrepreneur, she's a magician!"

"YOU WENT TOO FAR this time, Jane!" Audrey lamented, as she wedged in beside Jane at the main counter to ring up another sale. Now that Jane's tummy had expanded even beyond the chunky floor supervisor's, the space at the register was intolerably tight. The whole floor seemed cramped at the moment, as the basement's noon-hour influx of customers had developed into a suffocating crush.

Jane winked into Audrey's distressed face. "Too many commissions for you?" she whispered back with glee.

"My dogs are barkin'," Audrey insisted in a hiss.

"We are featuring sheer nighties from Lingerie in a package deal with a jar of chocolate paste from Gourmet Foods,"

Jane needlessly reminded her. "Feet should not be referred to as dogs."

Audrey's bosom heaved under her green knit dress. "Yeah, yeah, I know. For the duration of the special, all body parts are sensual instruments." She leaned over to punch in a double sale for a young blonde in a sober, skirted suit, her mouth close to Jane's ear. "Who'da ever guessed all the career gals working here in the city were budding sex kittens?" Jane smiled demurely at the customer, carefully folding the purchase into a nice bag. "And who'da ever thought of putting that innocent chocolate paste to such erotic use?" Audrey added in a cackle. "Kid, you're dynamite!"

Jane smiled fondly into space as she thought back to her wedding night, when she'd impulsively creamed her own breasts with decorator frosting. That's where the specific idea had emerged from.

"It really wasn't all that clever, Aud," she claimed airily. "All the buyers from all our departments now understand that I'm the person in line for the Baron crown, and are constantly pitching me ideas for intriguing new products. All of them want to be noticed before the department renovations begin, so that I'll consider them first in line for change."

"Well, I am mighty glad that I have you first!" Audrey proclaimed with pleasure.

"We make a wonderful team," Jane enthused, giving her friend's arm a squeeze.

"Ah-ah-ah," Audrey sang out as she gazed across the crowded floor. "Your Little Sir is just stepping out of the second elevator."

Jane nerves skidded at the sight of her strong handsome husband, striding along the aisle with long quick steps. He shone with West Coast sophistication, dressed in crisp black and white, with his layered bleached hair clipped neatly over his collar.

And she was so Midwest, she suddenly realized with dismay; rounded with pregnancy, dressed in a bright blue maternity dress. She'd altogether given up trying to squeeze into any of her regular clothing, opting for loose light-cotton garments most comfortable in the humid heat.

Four months pregnant and looking every bit of it. She'd expanded dramatically during their three-and-a-half week separation. What would he think when he saw her? How could she possibly stand up against the lanky California girls he dealt with in his work? Women like Nicole, who no doubt worked on their bodies with religious zeal. That was the sort of woman he'd been attracted to all these years.

Perhaps the stress would be too much for him. Not only was she adding to his responsibilities with the child, but she was losing her attractive shape in the process. She'd foolishly put those realities on the back burner while he was away. It had been easy to play the good-humored temptress on the telephone, through their express-mail messages, but reality was about to intrude.

Jane lifted her chin a fraction, forcing a welcoming smile as a foreign shyness engulfed her. She wouldn't step out from behind the counter. That would postpone the moment of truth!

Greg was shocked at the number of chattering women milling around the central display stand at the base of the escalator. His impressive height gave him a bird's-eye view above their heads. Apparently Jane was running a special on nighties. Transparent nighties in bold shades. Several varieties were on exhibit on plaster torsos. Some had fringe, some had lace, some had considerably less. There was a sign he couldn't clearly read, next to a pile of jars.

The sexy merchandise made his blood boil for her. It had been almost a whole month since he'd touched her, made sweet love to her. He couldn't help imagining her in one of those skimpy scraps of nylon, lush with his child.

Greg moved on toward the counter until he was close enough to connect with Janey. To make direct contact with her glittery sapphire eyes. Even if all the women in the room had been wearing the featured special, it wouldn't have diverted him for a second.

Those eyes. Those lovely captivating eyes full of mysteries and promises could keep him riveted from any other temptations.

"Welcome to seduction junction!" Audrey bellowed in blunt greeting, taking a customer's purchases over the counter. "You take five, Jane. The part-time stockers can ring some of these ladies up on the other counters."

"Hi, darling," Jane said on a tentative note just above the hum of music and voices.

Greg expected Jane to scurry out from behind the glass case, but she did not. He felt compelled to step in between two middle-aged women digging through a bin of scarves. "Hi, yourself." He reached over to push a dark tendril off her forehead.

Did she flinch at his touch? Greg clearly sensed a hesitation in her manner. But it seemed impossible. He'd spoken to her yesterday, right after he'd made the journey from Heathrow to LAX. She'd been absolutely fine. With his absence, his impending arrival. Everything had been right.

So what had gone wrong?

Greg's finger skidded down her cheek as he searched her face for a clue. Perhaps he was imagining it. She was rocky emotionally because of the pregnancy. And this madhouse down here had to be trying.

"Let's take Audrey's advice, honey," he murmured. "Take five."

"I can't!" she protested nervously. "I mean—I shouldn't."

She dropped her attention to the tumble of scarves the customers had left on the counter, but Greg gripped her fingers in his to still them. "C'mon, Janey," he urged intensely. "I've missed you so."

Missed the old her, she silently amended, leaning into the counter to further conceal her belly.

Audrey sidled back up to her before Greg could get in another word. "So has Jane explained her ingenious sales campaign?" she asked, a teasing gleam in her beady eyes.

Greg cleared his throat. "No, she hasn't. But it certainly seems a hit."

Audrey elbowed Jane in the ribs. "Tell the man, dearie."

Once Audrey moved back to the register, Jane held up one of the sheer nighties. "These come in a rainbow of colors," she said, coloring herself.

"Well, I guess that is a leap for the Emporium's modest underwear department," he said with a chuckle. "No wonder you didn't want Dad's interference."

Jane cracked a smile herself. "Well, there is a lot of profit potential for this sort of thing. And the buyer from Ladies' Foundations got a wonderful deal on them."

"So what's this stuff?" Greg asked, picking up a jar of the chocolate paste from a pyramid display at his elbow. "Isn't this from the gourmet section?"

"Yes, it's a gimmicky combination I put together, the lingerie and the candy."

"Wedding-night inspired," he wagered with a wolfish grin.

Jane's breath caught in her throat under his lustful gaze. She knew what he was going to say next. Oh, why hadn't they sponsored this promotion last week while he was still tucked away in some English village?

"I believe I'd like to purchase one of these sets myself," he declared, turning to eye the display behind him. "I'll take a red one, in the teddy style." He set a jar of chocolate on the glass between them. "Wrap it up and put it on my account, please."

Jane bit her lip. "I think there's something you ought to see first."

"Oh yeah?" His mouth crooked boyishly. "Another surprise?"

"Yeah." She took a deep steadying breath and launched herself around the counter. She marched right up beside him, her flowing blue dress billowing around her generous form.

Greg's eyes widened as they settled on her expanding abdomen. "Wow."

"See what I mean?" she whispered haltingly. "I can't, I wouldn't fit—" She broke off helplessly.

His hand stole down to the swell, gently caressing her tummy over the polished-cotton fabric of her maternity dress.

"Well?" she asked in a squeak.

Greg's mouth went dry as he sought to find the words. "I thought— My book—"

"I'm not the size four you left behind," she finished for him in a mumble. Four months along was more like it.

"I thought it would take longer to reach this point," he admitted, rubbing her gently but persistently, as though expecting her to deflate.

"You hate the way I look," she openly fretted.

"No, no," he hastily argued. "It's just so much more real to me now."

Her mouth curved hopefully. "Really?"

A tall, wiry old woman with yellowed hair and a Baron's clear shopping sack full of the practical toiletries paused to eavesdrop with open concern. "Is everything all right?"

"It certainly is, ma'am," Greg swiftly assured with a broad smile. "This lovely lady is bearing my child."

The woman set back on her heel with a humph. "Ah, well then, sir, I suggest you marry her without delay."

Jane flushed in embarrassment, her black lashes sweeping her cheekbones.

"We are very married," he turned to tell the woman succinctly.

With a doubtful snort and a whisk of her bag, she flounced toward a register at the opposite counter.

Greg took Jane by the elbow and ushered her over to a quiet corner near the rest rooms. He sat her down on a vinyl chair, taking her hands in his for inspection. "Honey, where's your wedding ring?"

"It's a little snug, so I haven't been able to wear it," she reluctantly confessed.

"Already?" he blurted out in complaint.

Jane snatched her hands back, exploding with pent-up emotion. "Wow? Already?" she drilled under her breath. "I knew you'd be disappointed, Greg. I can't fit into one of these little nylon numbers anymore, so I'm not what you want, what you've always expected from your playmates!"

The charge stung his ego and his heart. "I don't feel that way!"

"Well, the first thing you wanted to do was buy one for me!"

"Because I've missed you," he assured. "Because I thought it would be fun."

"Maybe I'm not going to be any fun anymore," she retorted.

Anger simmered beneath his look of disbelief. "This is ridiculous. I raced home like an eager teenager, I've missed you so. And this is what I'm faced with."

Her eyes shimmered with furious tears. "Just go, Greg."

He shrugged in stiff bewilderment. "I may as well, before I make things worse."

JANE WAS WATCHING television in bed back at the condo later on that evening, a pepperoni pizza before her on a tray, when she heard the latch turn in the front door. Recalling that everyone from Sir to Mabel to Grimes had a copy of the key to the Barons' downtown home, she set the tray aside and scrambled off the bed and out to the living room. She stopped short at the sight of Greg entering the dimly lit room, still dressed in his suit, a stuffed animal under his arm.

"Hi. I wondered . . . if it was you."

His head snapped up as he scanned her budding figure clothed only in one of his larger white T-shirts. His pregnant bride had never looked as radiant and inviting as she did at that very moment, with her hair shiny black and her limbs lost in the cotton-knit top. Of course, convincing her of the fact seemed like an insurmountable challenge.

"I brought something for the baby," he ventured softly, making the brown stuffed bear dance in his hands. "A whole different kind of teddy, one bound to keep me out of trouble. For you see, with this little guy, one size fits all."

"Oh, Greg!" she exclaimed with a mixture of relief and despair. "I don't know whether to hug you or strangle you!"

He closed the space between them. "I didn't mean anything this afternoon. And I still don't quite understand what happened between us."

She sighed hard, fingering his lapel. "I was afraid that you wouldn't find me attractive anymore. And that seemed to be the case, Greg."

"That's ridiculous, honey," he admonished in a purr. "You're the biggest turn-on a man could hope for. With or without child."

"Well, I've changed a lot since you left," she argued. "I can't stand in comparison to the women you deal with in Los Angeles. They're too lean, too tan, too—limber!"

"I don't find any of my co-workers attractive in the way I do you," he insisted.

"Ah, but you zoomed in, expecting me to squeeze into one of those nighties! It seemed to validate my worst fears. Then you were peeved about your mother's ring not fitting me...." She shook her head in helplessness. "I felt I'd just inflated another ten inches from head to toe!"

"That old woman made me angry, telling me to marry you," he confessed with a rueful turn of his mouth. "All I saw was that that beautiful stone of my mother's wasn't on your finger anymore, and I had to assure a stranger that I was indeed looking after the mother of my child." He lifted his broad, tailored shoulders. "Guess it was just too much, honey. After all the whizzing around the world I've done in the name of my job. I was just stressed out, at the end of my rope."

And there were the secrets she and Sir shared, about their high blood pressure, their childbirth classes, their in-store schemes, and hell-only-knew what else. He had felt left out.

Greg had had all afternoon to ponder his new circumstances, how he'd gotten to this point.

He was the one who'd left them. His absence was legitimate, but that didn't stop time from marching on without him. He'd fought so hard to stand his ground with Sir and Jane. Now, to his amazement, he felt he was standing over the center of an earthquake. The foundation he'd taken for granted all these years in his self-centered existence was crumbling into an unexplored territory.

"You still look very strained," she bluntly observed, eyeing him suspiciously. "Are you really glad to be back?"

"I want you more than ever!" he exclaimed vehemently, causing her to jump a little. "Look, honey, it's the bond between you and Dad that's got me a little uptight. You've always been close, but now the division between you seems almost seamless!"

She laughed with release. "Oh, Greg, is that all?"

"It's something big to me. You took him to your childbirth classes—in my place! Why didn't you wait for me, honey?"

"There was an opening so I took it," she babbled on contritely. "I was darn lucky to get in. It's during the noon hour and very popular with the working women here downtown." In reality she had wanted to get most of it over with in the first trimester, when her bogus due date would be accepted by the instructor without question.

"So there's one class left for me, then?"

"Yes, next Friday."

He nodded with satisfaction. "Good."

"About Amanda's ring, Greg," Jane anxiously broke into his thoughts. "I don't want to tamper with it, enlarge it temporarily. It's always pleased me that she and I were of the same build and coloring. I figure she managed somehow while carrying you, so I shall, too."

"That was one subject I enjoyed speaking to Dad about," he intimated with a smile. "And he had just the answer." Greg dipped a hand into his jacket pocket and extracted a small velvet box.

Jane took the box from his extended palm. She cracked open the cover to find a simple gold band wedged on end inside.

"It's nothing fancy," he hastened to admit. "Just a symbol, really, to ward off the old biddies like that one in the basement today."

She tipped her face to his, her eyes crinkled in appreciation. "It's just right, Greg. Perfect for me."

"As you're perfect for me," he murmured in the curve of her ear. "Here, let me slip that on you."

Jane took the bear from his arms and extended her left hand.

He eased the band on her ring finger. "That should feel quite comfortable."

"Yes," she agreed breathlessly. "Just loose enough for a little more expansion."

He kissed her temples lightly. "You've never been more attractive to me than you are at this moment, honey, I promise."

She extended her lip poutily. "Don't stretch it to the unbelievable!"

"I'm not!" he declared adamantly, angling an arm around her shoulders before she could twist away. "I'm just as surprised as you are by the new feelings. I've never given a pregnant woman a second glance before, never looked into a child's eyes and thought, yeah, I can be a parent." He held her gaze with raw candor. "But now, confronted with these things, I feel energized, excited, brand-new!" He drew her flush against his solid length, his voice growing husky. "As tough as this separation has been, it has given me a chance to examine where we are and what we have. I appreciate you more than ever."

"I hope you don't have to fly off every time you need to think!"

"Of course not," he assured with a chuckle. "The major self-exploration has to be over. And I would like you to put your fears to rest once and for all about other women," he said firmly.

"Prepared to have a hump inserted between your shoulders? Your nostrils widened? Your ears enlarged? Just how are we going take you away from the roving female eyes?"

He smiled faintly. "It's Nicole we're really discussing," he chided. "And it appears that she is finally making an effort at the dating game. She and Stephen Humphries have really hit it off."

"Really?" Elation danced in her eyes, despite her modulated voice.

"Truly. You should be able to relax on all counts now, go back to whatever you were doing." He looked around the dim, quiet room. "So what exactly was that?"

"Oh, I was in bed," she replied, nuzzling the bear's head under her chin.

His blond brows arched in surprise. "Already? I'm starving."

"No problem," she announced breezily, taking him by the hand.

Greg obediently trailed after her to the bedroom, aghast at the sight before him. Pizza and a half glass of milk on a lap tray, open bags of chips and pretzels, a bowl of melting ice cream. "The mattress looks like a smorgasbord, Janey!"

"It's okay," she grumbled, crawling across to her spot against the wall. "There's still room for you."

He winced as she snuggled back into place, setting the tray of pizza on her lap. He pulled back his side of the bedspread, to find it littered with crumbs and candy wrappers. The reasons for her accelerated expansion appeared to be right under his own covers! But the wiser man in him knew to keep his theory to himself.

She set the teddy between their pillows and lifted a wedge of pizza to her mouth. "C'mon, climb in."

Shaking his head, Greg peeled off his suit jacket and began to work at the knot in his tie. He stripped down to his briefs, slipped into some beige running shorts, and made another perusal of the bed. "If you don't mind, I think I'll pop out to the balcony and grill myself a fillet on the barbecue."

"Yum!" Jane squealed, dabbing her mouth with a napkin. "Tell you what, take the rest of this pizza back to the kitchen and stick it in the fridge. Oh, and hand me the TV remote before you go," she requested, gesturing to the twenty-five-inch set across the room in the wall-to-wall entertainment center. "It's on top of the *TV Guide*. Oh, heck, might as well give me the guide, too."

Greg delivered the items, wondering: Was she expecting a steak, too? Would she be upset if he asked? Jane clicked on the television set and dug into a sack of pretzels.

"Anything else you need?" he asked, fishing from the doorway.

She tossed her thick wavy mane over her shoulder. "Nope. Just make mine medium rare."

Jane settled back on the pillows as a sitcom blared to life on the screen. She set the teddy bear in her lap, squeezing its belly with her thumbs. He was so adorable. And what a thoughtful gift. As unpretentious as the gold band.

A sudden jolt of realization caused her heart to plummet. Greg would absolutely die when he walked into their new nursery full of stuffed animals. It would be a lethal blow, for sure, to discover that his father had upstaged him again, dwarfed his poor teddy with a population worthy of Noah's Ark!

She released a shaky breath. Thank heavens she hadn't pulled him in there without thinking. It would have destroyed their reunion without doubt!

Greg deserved the chance to be on record for presenting his baby with its first bear.

Something would have to be done about all those other toys before Greg tripped over them. Luckily he paid little attention to that extra room tucked away at the end of the hall. It was an extra wheel of sorts, the third bedroom in line behind this master suite and the spacious guest room. She couldn't let Sir gain another inch of footing at Greg's expense. She was convinced that in his own way, Greg was as fragile as his own unborn child.

11

"WHAT DO YOU MEAN, you're going away with Sir?"

Jane took the news of Mabel's trip to Brainerd with Clark without grace the following morning. Greg was waiting for her in the living room, set to walk the five blocks over to the Emporium for a full day of work. She'd fled back to the bedroom on the pretense of searching for a pair of more comfortable shoes to match her magenta shirtdress and black leggings, when in fact she was putting out an S.O.S. call for a stuffed-animal pickup.

Seated on the edge of the bed, she couldn't help but send furtive looks back to the doorway, just waiting for Greg to appear and tune in to what she was doing. She couldn't help but make the call under his nose, with the hope that Mabel and Sir could come remove their stuffed zoo today, during working hours. That would leave her free to show Greg the beginnings of the nursery, with its fresh wallpaper and refinished dresser from her own childhood bedroom. She planned to set his teddy bear atop the dresser, make a big deal out of how the toy matched the wallpaper.

"Surely you don't have a problem with appearances, with Clark and I being unmarried and all," Mabel clucked over the wire. "I didn't raise you to be a ninny."

"No, no," she said in return, easing her feet into some black leather flats. "I just needed to speak to you about a favor."

"Can't it wait until next week?" Mabel wondered aloud. "We're leaving today—"

Jane's forehead furrowed with determination. "What time are you leaving?"

"Janey! Is this some sort of emergency? And why are you whispering?"

"No, not in the literal sense," she felt compelled to confess, bowing her head to rub her temples. "I just need some help with the nursery. It's nothing for you to worry about. I suppose we can deal with it when you return."

"If it's nothing urgent, dear, I really must go," she announced gaily. "Clark and Grimes have just pulled up in the Town Car."

Jane leapt off the mattress with phone in hand, whirling to find Greg hovering in the doorway. "Sorry, Grandma, but I can't chat anymore. Greg's waiting."

"But isn't that what I just said?" Mabel protested. "With Clark's and Grimes's names in place of Greg's?"

"If you find any fudge in those small tourist traps, bring me home several pounds," Jane improvised in a rush.

"Nuts?"

"I am not!" Jane squealed.

"In the fudge," Mabel clarified with a sigh. "I don't know where you get your tizziness from, Jane. But I suggest you work on controlling it."

"Sure, sure. Bye now, sweetie. Have a good time." She hung up the phone with a humph. "That was Mabel."

"So I gathered." Greg wedged his solid shoulder against the doorframe, shoving his hands into the pockets of his gray linen trousers. "Is everything all right?"

"Dandy. Did you know they're going on their trip first thing this morning?"

"Yes. But I figured I was the last to know, as usual." He sauntered into the room, surveying her feet to see if she'd found another pair of shoes. She was so glad she'd gone through the motions of doing so!

"I just wanted to check in with her," she lilted in explanation. "Caught her as she was about to walk out the door."

Greg paused before the freestanding mirror, fiddling with his black tie. "I wonder if I should trade this one for a rusty stripe."

"Oh, I dunno." She rose and did a head roll to relieve the stiffness in her neck.

"I keep a rack of ties in the spare room closet," he mused in indecision.

Jane froze in place with her hands on her hips. She'd considered removing all of his extra clothing from that closet, but figured there was no rush. Now he wanted to get in there. In all the time they'd known each other, she'd never seen him enter that room for a doggone thing!

"You know, I really like that black tie," she hastily claimed with a sugary smile.

"A minute ago, you didn't care," he asserted in confusion.

"Rust will clash with my magenta dress," she blurted out in protest.

He paused. "Yeah, guess it would."

Jane released a low slow breath of relief as he ushered her through the doorway.

"We don't want to clash at all today," he said excitedly.

"Why not today, Greg?"

"Because we're giving a presentation together. I've called a managers' meeting for the noon hour. I've arranged for catering from the Emporium restaurant and we're going to get down to this renovation business."

Jane paused in the building corridor as Greg set the dead bolt. "But Sir wanted to take things slow, watch how things go in the basement first."

"Janey, he'll never move without a shove. And the bank has made it more than clear to me that he absolutely must do so before the New Year."

She frowned. "I know you're right. But he's so charismatic on the job, that I sometimes forget that he really doesn't mean to make any swift changes down the road."

"All I want to do is take this time for some candid discussion with the managers," Greg assured, taking her arm as they started down the corridor. "Those surveys you put together are great. We'll pass those out at lunch, encourage everyone to brainstorm, fill us in on the problems they see in their own departments."

"Sir liked the surveys too, promised to use them sometime soon."

"That's his legendary stall with employees," Greg reminded. "Things were different when Dad was really down, of course. Humoring him was necessary. But his vitality has returned and he's more than capable of taking on our challenges." He tapped her upturned nose with a light finger. "And let's face it, there will never be a time when you're more influential than you are right now. He finally has you in the family legally and you're producing an heir. We've got to move immediately!"

"You're using me as a secret weapon!" she scoffed.

"Yes, of course!" Greg confessed with pride. "But it's for a good cause."

"Yeah, I admit that. But you're insinuating the shine will eventually wear off," she accused saucily, reaching out to push the elevator button.

"Honey, we all fall into routines, come to accept even the most joyous of circumstances. Dad's bound to step off his cloud a little bit once the baby's here. If it's any consolation, I haven't seen him this happy in years. You bring out the best in him the way Mom used to do."

"You're sneaky," she grumbled with a sock to his arm. But even as the words tumbled from her mouth, she knew she beat him in the devious department, hands down.

"I DON'T CONDONE this sort of conspiracy for one instant!"

Desmond Nibling had taken one look at the survey set before him at the managers' luncheon and leapt to his feet in protest.

Greg smiled thinly from the podium at the front of the meeting room, wishing he could grab the head of Toys by his beaky nose and hurl him out the delivery door, once and for all. "This can't be a surprise to you, Nibs. I haven't been around for a month, but it's my understanding that the store is humming with the buzz of change. That most of you have been pitching Mrs. Baron with ideas," he added. "You want to be noticed for your innovation and clever merchandising—"

"I do not!" Nibling bellowed, causing peals of laughter to ripple through the room.

"You do not want to be noted for being innovative and clever?" Greg challenged sharply.

"I like things as they are," Nibling corrected in a bluster.

Greg looked down at Jane, seated at the table right in front of him. She was still smarting from what Nibling had done to her. The hypocrite had condemned her hands-on display of the playground equipment, then greedily reaped the rewards. Greg had been as patient with his father's policies as he could be. But this man just didn't quit. And it would be Greg's pleasure to finally pull in the reins on him. "It's my understanding that you're more than willing to gain from clever selling," he cautioned tersely. "So I feel compelled to warn you that anyone who feels opposed to the policies I've outlined today should hand in a resignation, or step down to a lesser position of authority. If Baron's is to survive, we must move forward with the times."

Nibling gritted his teeth, his egg-shaped face cherry red. "Why, your father likes the old ways. He wouldn't stand for—"

"My father has made it more than clear that he intends for my wife, Jane, to succeed him as head of Baron's Emporium," Greg interrupted sternly. "I can't think of a more progressive vision than that. I suggest you accustom yourself to the new reality, Mr. Nibling. Now, time is limited, and we have many points to cover on the survey. If you want to argue the issues, I suggest you make an appointment with Mrs. Baron for another time."

Nibling lurched forward with a glare. "I will do no such thing! I quit!"

Applause traversed the room as Desmond Nibling staunchly weaved through the round tables toward the exit.

"I'm certain your expression of approval is solely for my wife's new position," Greg smoothly ascertained, shuffling through the papers before him. Laughter and applause intermingled for the next few minutes, leaving everyone with a relaxed sense of camaraderie.

Jane gazed up into Greg's eyes with loving respect, to find much of the same reflecting back at her. He'd taken on Nibling for her, addressed that unfinished business and brought home justice. He could have skirted Nibs again, backed down again, but he'd forced Nibling to comply or walk. The old sorehead had made himself redundant out of sheer pettiness.

For the first time since their marriage of convenience had started, Jane felt that Greg had come to regard her as a permanent member of the Baron family. And she felt just the tiniest prick of guilt, that while he was busy defending her honor, she'd nibbled away at his strawberry tart and ice cream.

JANE SPENT THE DURATION of the week touring the departments with a clipboard full of the filled-out surveys, interviewing each manager on his or her own turf, taking copious notes on her findings.

Greg divided his time in smaller allotments. He discussed all of Jane's findings, offering advice and support. And he spent a lot of time back at the condo, lining up a cameraman and sound recordist for an educational film on pilot safety, fund-raising for a piece on substance abuse for a St. Paul school district, and hammering out the final details for the return trip to England. He intended to bring along a larger production unit than usual for the village tour. After a long powwow, he and Kevin had decided to expand the budget to include a second cameraman to assist the director of photography, and a sound crew rather than a single recordist.

When he wasn't immersed in either business, he was reading everything he could get his hands on concerning prenatal classes. He'd missed so much in the first three sessions and wanted to be on top of it all.

By Friday noon he was ready for his trip over to the YWCA.

Jane was more nervous than he, taking quick little steps along the crowded city sidewalks. He'd come to realize that her outfits were almost like a uniform, roomy shirts of satin or cotton, paired with stretchy leggings and comfortable flat shoes. And she looked absolutely enchanting in the clothing. A plump little elf. Despite her ravenous appetite, she was still well proportioned and graceful. Apparently her doctor had condoned her continuing on with her aerobics class in a modified form. And Jane was always stretching on the carpet like a supple kitten. Whatever she was doing obviously kept her in good shape.

As they approached the glass entrance of the Y, Jane caught his arm and pulled him aside under the awninged entrance. "There's something I think you should know—"

"Hey," he crooned. "I've researched this deal thoroughly. I'll make you proud."

"No, it's nothing like that," she objected with a cringe. "It's just that Sir sort of stole the show for three weeks running."

Greg rolled his eyes. "I should've guessed! Did he tell everyone he would be your coach at the hospital, as well?"

"Well, he skirted the issue with some fine footwork," she confessed with a weak smile.

"The old goat wouldn't be able to come within ten yards of a real birth," Greg assured her with a flash of indulgent humor. "But leave it to him to lap up the glory."

Jane giggled. "I think he was quite relieved that you returned when you did. They're showing a video of a real birth today."

"He would've made Grimes come in his place, I imagine."

"I just wanted to warn you that his absence will be noted immediately."

Greg kept his spine erect as they entered the lobby and veered off down the hallway on the left. He was walking into a room already worked over by his father—no less than three times! He was the second fiddle all over again. But his time would come. When his baby popped into the world with a lusty cry, he would be the first Baron that child would see.

The classroom was already full of expectant parents. They were all mingling in small clusters—until they spotted Jane with her younger coach. The noise faded and all eyes riveted to them.

"Hello!" Jane called out merrily. "This is Greg, my husband."

Greetings were exchanged. Greg noticed a ripe curiosity in their eyes. And Jane seemed to know all of them so well. But it was natural, he reasoned. The classes were bound to touch on intimate topics. And the exercises Jane did at night involved some odd positions. To be fair, the feeling in the room could be best described as a friendly closeness.

The group leader, a brunette in her early thirties, was the first to ask where good old Clark was.

"He's in Brainerd," Jane replied. "You know, he really wouldn't have been up to the tape of the live birth you're planning to show today, Amelia," she confided with a sigh, obviously trying to put her charming father-in-law in perspective for all of them.

"Dad is an old-fashioned man," Greg agreed, flattered by the protective shield his wife had dropped over him. "He might've come in a pinch, but he would've closed his eyes a lot."

"Well, it's wonderful that you could join us for this final class, Greg," Amelia enthused, with a glance at her watch. "I imagine we'd better get started. Lots to cover. We have our regular conditioning exercises, my lecture on what to do when labor begins. At the forefront, of course, we have the tape of the birth." She instructed everyone to gather around the large television at the front of the room and turned back to Greg with a smile. "I hope you won't judge my video for style. It's very amateurish."

"I'm not here as a producer, but as a father," he politely assured.

Greg was in the habit of judging all films by his high standards, but discovered that this time he was far more interested in the birth itself than he was in the lighting, sound and camera angles. Though the video was rough, it was powerful. Simply because it was the record of a miracle.

And Jane was giving him a miracle of his own. It shamed him to think of how upset he'd been—first when he'd erroneously believed her pregnant, then when it turned out to be for real. Being a parent was a privilege.

As the class progressed toward the exercise period near the end, Jane noted that Greg was treating her like the most delicate crystal. Especially now, during the touch-relaxation phase. As she and the other mothers were practicing their "roving body check" to relieve stress from head to toe, Greg was hovering on his knees beside her, frantic with every rotation she made. As she moved her legs, arms and chest in the eight-part countdown, he fretted like a frightened old maid.

She couldn't believe this was the same sexual marvel that had shared her bed last night!

But she understood. It was all in his beautiful silver eyes. He was not only intellectually in tune with their circumstances, but he was now also emotionally connected with what was happening.

Jane said little as the class broke up and people said goodbye for the last time. Luckily they had a store to run and couldn't linger on to discuss nitpicky stuff like due dates. She'd given them her false due date at the beginning and was exceedingly grateful that no one had commented about her growth over the past month.

Greg's awe was still intact as they hit the street. There was a stronger, far more powerful bond between them as they moved down the sidewalk. Greg had her hand encapsulated in his own like a precious flower petal. She knew better than to ask him if he was glad he'd come. His joy was written across his angled features. But as he watched over her at a red light, she did ask him if he'd learned anything new.

"Oh, yeah, honey," he purred, rubbing the base of her spine for a brief moment. "Especially about myself. You're giving me the greatest gift a man can get. And I'm grateful. Extremely grateful."

Jane floated the rest of the way back to the Bargain Basement.

CLARK AND MABEL returned Sunday night. Greg had taken Jane to an art fair in Minneapolis, so they didn't receive Sir's message on the machine until after ten o'clock.

"It's too late to call, Greg," Jane declared, already peeling off her shawl as she backed toward the study doorway.

Greg stared down at the telephone for a long pensive moment, stroking his stubbled chin. "He already knows things are brewing at the store," he stated with certainty. "He probably had some messages waiting for him on his machine, and naturally went through them before calling here."

"From the likes of Nibling, for instance?"

Greg turned to regard her soberly. "Yes. And several other of his old-time employees. Even the ones who approve would have wanted to speak to him."

Jane pressed her hands into the small of her achy spine and slowly pulled her shoulders back.

Greg's forehead furrowed in concern. "You okay?"

"Oh, yes, just exhausted," she confessed on a yawn. "This baby of ours never lets me forget it's around."

"That is a trait from the Haley side, all right," he teased. "Persistent grandstand plays for attention."

"A charming trait."

As her mouth curved playfully, he moved close to cover it with his own. Massaging the sides of her tummy through her eyelet dress, he released a deep, satisfied moan. "Let's go to bed. I'll help you with your relaxation exercises."

She braced her hands on the expanse of his chest to keep him from scooping her up. "Maybe you should call him tonight."

He shook his head with certainty. "Missing his call was most likely for the best. He said he'll be at his desk first thing in the morning, in that summons tone of his. We'll lead with you tomorrow, as planned, my pretty," he growled seductively, pushing aside her mane of raven hair to nibble at her neck. "Just like me, he just can't say no to you."

12

JANE WAS TORN BETWEEN presenting an image of sweetness or power the following morning as she dressed for her meeting with Sir. She eventually reached a visual balance with an uncompromising black skirt, topped with a silk blouse in a shade of dusty pink that Sir would adore.

It was raining, so they drove to work in her Saturn. As fun as Greg's sports car was, Jane found it increasingly uncomfortable to ride in. And she wanted Greg to become more accustomed to larger vehicles. Once the baby came, she wanted to buy a minivan.

Greg pulled up at the front entrance on Cedar Street.

"Wish me luck," she said with a steadying breath.

He leaned over to kiss her cheek. "Maybe we should do this together."

That was the last thing she wanted! But she couldn't allow him to zone in on her skittishness. She dismissed the idea with a sweep of her hand. "I love having you as my safety net, darling, but being his successor, I may as well become accustomed to hashing things out with him."

"Yeah, I suppose." He reached into her open tan trench coat to set his hand on the silken pink curve of her blouse. "Just keep that tummy out at all times. Remind him of who he's dealing with."

"As if I could do anything else!" she retorted, feeling every ounce of her cargo as she eased out onto the sidewalk.

Jane reached the seventh-floor suite of offices to find Sir behind his desk as promised, dressed in a dark brown suit and a pale blue shirt. He was pouring himself a cup of coffee from an insulated pot on the desk.

"Good morning!" she greeted brightly, sliding off her coat.

Sir nodded as she slipped it onto a hanger in the closet. "Crummy morning. Weather-wise, I mean."

"Oh, the dark clouds are clearing off," she countered with a grin.

"Always looking for the silver lining, aren't you?"

"Naturally," she lilted, accepting the cup he slid across the desk.

"It's decaf," he hastily assured.

"I hope so," she murmured. "For your own sake as well as mine."

His eyes crinkled at the corners as he studied her. "How are you feeling?"

"I've been on pins and needles since you left!" she confided.

He steepled his fingers under his narrow chin. "Can't say I'm surprised. With all of your causes."

She lifted her cup to her lips. Sipping the steamy brew, she inadvertently noted that he'd been studying the departmental surveys. Between his informants and those papers, Sir undoubtedly had a clear picture of what she'd been up to in his absence. But all of that would have to wait, for now. She had a far more important mission on her mind.

"You happen to be the one who's put me in a prickly spot," she hastened to inform him.

His lined mouth dropped open. "Me? I've been away!"

"Yes! You caused the trouble, then ran away!" she cried in complaint, clanking her cup against its saucer.

He balked under her fiery accusations. "I haven't run any-place in twenty years! And I've never backed away from trouble."

She nodded vigorously. "You've put me in a very precarious position with Greg."

His expression clouded in confusion and panic. "Dear daughter, what are you talking about?"

"Oh, bringing that parade of stuffed animals into the condo," she clarified in a huff. "I wanted to show him my handiwork in the spare room—with the wallpaper and the refinished dresser—and now I can't!"

He threw his hands up helplessly. "Why ever not?"

"Because you've upstaged him, that's why!"

"Janey, Janey, you never cease to amaze me. This is what you consider the priority of the day?"

"Yes, I do. Can't you see, it's Greg's turn to shine as a parent?"

"So let him shine," Clark proclaimed. "I'm not stopping him! Hell, I'm the one who strongly suggested he give it a try."

"I don't think you mean to upstage him," she asserted empathetically. "But take, for instance, the way you stepped into the birthing classes at the Y."

"You needed a coach!" he insisted defensively. "You asked me."

"Yes, I know," she conceded. "But you have a certain appeal that draws in strangers. Everyone wondered where you were at that last class, wondered why you didn't come back. It was tough on Greg." She paused for a calming breath. "It just seems that with Greg's busy schedule, he's coming in behind you in all of these preparations. You simply have to throttle back on your grandpa zeal, for your son's sake."

"So you don't think he can handle my stuffed animals?" he asked dolefully.

"He could have, if he hadn't chosen to present me with a single teddy bear," Jane explained. "The gesture meant the world to him, to be the first in line with a toy, to finally assert his position as the doting dad!"

"You're certainly determined to run interference for him."

"I have to help! He's so busy trying to be strong and capable, that he deals with most of this internally. Look how hard he's tried. He went along with the wedding you planned, tried to run the Emporium the way you wanted it run." Sir grunted at that last phrase, but she talked right over it. "And the way the employees call him Little Sir . . . why, it's ridiculous. Greg has made his mark in the world, attained recognition in his own field. Yet he yields to you and me in an effort to do the right thing."

Clark nodded, rubbing his chin. "True, that Little Sir stuff has become outdated. But he knows I respect him. And he approves of my collaboration with you. Obviously I've been doing my part to keep the status quo."

"Then you're willing to go over to the condo and remove all those animals," she gushed warmly, reaching across the blotter to give his bony wrist a quick squeeze.

He raised his eyes with a moan. "Oh, Jane."

"Mabel can help you," she pressed. "And perhaps Grimes."

"Grimes has the day off." He sent her a begrudging look. "Can't you just tell Greg you bought the toys?"

"No," she insisted firmly. "Greg has to see that teddy in place in the nursery. All alone."

"Oh, all right," he surrendered, rubbing his hands over his face.

Her small features brightened. "Now, about the store events—"

"Ah, the Emporium," he interrupted with mild sarcasm. "Nearly forgot all about it, didn't you?"

"No, of course not!" she scoffed, taking him seriously. "It's just that all our affairs, personal and business, intertwine into this great big jumble. And it seemed to me that Greg's feelings were at the top of today's list."

"Had a string of messages on my machine concerning your managers' meeting," he informed her with a sharper directness.

"I figured you would," Jane returned smoothly, keeping her chin high. "Thought I'd get the renovation ball rolling by accumulating some facts from the departments. You said there would be changes in the upcoming months, and by golly, I'm determined to gather all the information we need." He opened his mouth to speak, but she charged merrily on. "And it was good for employee morale. The managers were thrilled to express their ideas." She leaned back in her chair, a glitter in her blue eyes. "There is a mounting excitement in the store, Sir. There is a new hope for blockbluster sales figures. Larger commissions for ambitious people. Everyone wants to sell-sell-sell."

His jaw worked as he struggled to keep up with her line of patter. "You know I've been open to your ideas—"

"Of course you have!" she congratulated.

"But it isn't a race—"

"Ah, but in a way it is, Sir." She gave an apologetic smile. "The customers who are enjoying the new look of the basement are expecting the same sort of change throughout the store. And the employees are tired of losing customers to Audrey and me downstairs. Don't you see? This renovation deal is like a soaring rocket, picking up speed by the day." She sank back in her chair wearily.

"About the phone messages—"

"Now, weren't most of those calls positive?"

"Well, some of the older heads—"

"Nibling has a gut full of sour grapes," she complained. "And he quit under his own steam."

"Yes, I gathered that," Sir replied as she drew a breath. "He didn't care much for the idea of you taking on a position at my right."

"Hah! I'll bet he didn't. After the way he pushed me out of Toys!"

"Well, he has put in enough time at the Emporium to reap a good retirement package," Sir reasoned.

Jane bit her lip to suppress her glee. Nibling really was gone for good. "You know, Sir. I'd like to kick off the modernization project in Toys without delay. I know a lot about the department, having worked there for a while. And it's got such potential, a real showcase for our new ideas. It could be a real attention grabber like the basement's been." She fluttered her lashes at him.

He heaved his tailored chest. "All right. Have at it."

"I'll start by reconstructing that Plas-Tek equipment," she said, half to herself.

"With a change of costume, I imagine," he said wryly.

"Oh, you rogue!" she teased with a wave. "I'm not in any shape to tackle that slide in a tutu or anything else. I'll be taking on more of an overseer's position."

"Too darn bad," he murmured with a thin smile. "You're the best salesperson to ever walk these floors."

"You flatter me," she demurred.

"No, young lady, I do not," he rumbled in wonder. "So where is the proud papa-to-be now?"

"Oh, he had some errands to run," Jane answered, slowly rising from her chair with a firm grip on the armrests. "A trip to the cleaners and the dentist."

"What time would you like the animals picked up?" he inquired drolly.

"Oh, it doesn't matter," she airily assured, smoothing her pink blouse. "Just any time during working hours, I suppose. Greg plans to come back here before noon. I can keep him busy around here till closing time."

"Well, you go ahead and weave magic on the floor," he told her, picking up the telephone receiver. "I'll give Mabel a call and see how soon she can be ready. Though I imagine she's damn sick of me after our trip."

"Don't you dare start to underestimate that magnetism of yours." With a crooked grin, she waltzed out the door.

JANE WAS STILL IN the toy department as the noon hour approached. She was surprised when one of the young male clerks tracked her down in the game aisle to report that Greg was on the telephone. She ambled up to the main counter and picked up the receiver. "Greg? Where are you?"

"Hi, honey, I'm double-parked out front," he reported above the traffic noise.

"You're calling from the car phone? Why?"

"Because I'm taking you to lunch. Chinese."

"Oh?" she lilted with interest. "To tell you the truth, I haven't thought about food all morning."

His chuckle rippled the line. "What on earth could've taken a front seat to your appetite?"

"The revamping of Toys," she confided in a low, excited tone. "Nibling's gone for good. And I have Sir's blessing to forge on."

"Things must have gone well, then," he surmised with pleasure.

"Yes!"

"Well, grab your purse and come on down. We'll celebrate with double helpings."

"Don't move that car an inch!" Jane pushed the disconnect button, then called up to Sir's office. To her delight, he was not in, and not expected back until after three. That had to mean he was clearing those animals out for her. Without further delay, she grabbed her shoulder bag, had a word with the clerk in charge and zoomed toward the elevators.

"Why won't you tell me where we're going for lunch?" Jane demanded several minutes later as Greg eased the Saturn into traffic on Cedar.

"Because it's a surprise."

There were so many restaurants in the heart of downtown, that Jane was not troubled when he avoided the route to the freeway. But within a couple of blocks, a knot of suspicion grew in her belly. "You aren't taking us to the condo, are you?"

"You caught me!" he confessed with chuckle.

"But there's no food at the condo," she sputtered. "Not real good old American Chinese food like you promised!"

"I'm having it delivered," he informed her. When she remained distraught, he grew defensive. "I figured you'd be thrilled to have the chance to slip off your shoes, eat in bed the way you like."

"I'd like to eat in a restaurant for a change. The one on Fifth Street has wonderful lemon chicken."

"Sorry, honey, but I already ordered the food. It's going to be a close shave, beating the deliveryman."

And a closer shave avoiding the take-away crew. Her heart hammered as she envisioned the clash. But there was nothing she could do but hope for the best.

Just as she feared, the front door of the condo was slightly ajar. Walking down the corridor a few steps ahead of Greg gave her the advantage of seeing it first. She barged inside before he could take note and suspect trouble.

"Why, Clark! Mabel!" she greeted cheerily. "What a nice surprise!"

Mabel froze in the center of the sun-drenched living room, her arm around the stuffed giraffe's throat. "It is?"

"Hello, kids," Sir interceded jovially, assessing the problem faster than his partner in deception.

"Dad." Greg regarded the pair of seniors huddled around the menagerie of stuffed animals in amazement. "What are you doing?"

"You know, Janey, you were right about the weather turning bright," Clark declared. "Seemed like too nice a day to stay cooped up in the office."

"So you decided to play zoo?" Greg surmised sardonically, folding his arms across his solid chest.

Jane cringed. Another ten minutes and her coconspirators would have been safely in an elevator with the whole darn kingdom!

"The Chinese food arrived," Clark announced. "More than the two of you could ever eat."

"Don't bet on it," Greg said dryly.

Mabel cleared her throat, righting the giraffe on its base. "I'm sure you're wondering what all of this is about. Well, I can explain."

"Really, Grandma?" Jane queried with a look of warning.

She patted her chest above the ruffled neckline of her floral print dress. "I'm more than certain I can. Given time—"

"What the hell," Sir interrupted, causing Jane to gasp. "It's a surprise, son. Janey told me you brought home a teddy bear, and Mabel and I got to thinking it should have some company."

"Yes," Mabel chimed in with open delight. "We just arrived with these furry friends. That's what I was trying to say."

"Spoiling the baby already," Jane chided teasingly, nudging Greg. "Isn't that just like these two!"

Greg rocked on his heels, his features narrowed in confusion. "But why sneak over here? Why not just show up when we're at home?"

"Ah..." Mabel's puffy face clouded in doubt. "That's a tougher one."

"Because of me," Jane announced in a rush of inspiration.

Greg balked with a laugh. "You, Jane?"

"Well, yes, let me show you." Jane grabbed him by the arm and led him back to the spare room.

Greg followed her into the center of the new nursery, taking in the bright teddy-bear wallpaper and the refinished dresser. He whirled on his wife, his face full of wonder. "You did this, honey?"

"Yes, while you were on your trip," Jane explained. "They helped me." She gestured to the senior pair hovering in the doorway, obviously waiting to see how much Greg would swallow.

He planted his hands on his hips and slowly shook his head. "But why the secrecy?"

"Well, it isn't really finished," she faltered, shifting from one foot to another.

Greg's face melted into boyish delight right before their eyes. "That's cute, the way you put my bear on top of the dresser."

Sir winked at Jane behind Greg's back. His message read: "Hook, line and sinker."

They all gathered in the kitchen to have lunch. They ate family-style, each taking samples from all the large steaming white cartons full of chow mein, rice, egg rolls and chicken; washing it down with some of Jane's favorite tea.

Greg dabbed his mouth with a paper napkin halfway through the meal. "This seems as good a time as any for me to make an announcement," he began with pleasant firmness. Three sets of eyes skirted around the table, then came to rest on him warily. "I have had my fill of surprises from you people—enough to last me a good long while."

Mabel made a peeping sound. "I was rather hoping you liked surprises, Gregory. Weren't you, Jane?"

Jane's eyes measured Greg, then Mabel, then Greg again. He meant business. His hooded gaze sent a laserlike message of intent. She offered him a wan smile. "Well, as it happens, I was sort of hoping you did like surprises, darling."

"No, what I like is equilibrium," he insisted, forking some brown rice.

"Oh, everybody here knows you've had to bend some, these months," Sir philosophized with a shrug. "Big deal. Your life is in transition, from footloose bachelor to husband and father."

"Yes, but I feel like I'm stumbling through a fun house," he complained. "It's nothing that can't be easily resolved, of course," he assured evenly. "I'm simply tired of having things sprung on me. I've taken the wedding, the baby, Jane's promotion in the store, missing the childbirth classes all in stride." He gazed over the open containers to find fallen faces. "I know this nursery full of creatures doesn't seem like an earth-rocking shock to you, but I'm simply tired of your guileful methods. A little plain talk up front never hurt anybody. Let's give it a try, okay?"

Jane nodded in understanding, but her pulse was leaping in panic. He would be so angry when he came to realize that not only was she pregnant when he'd first been told she was, but also that Sir had known the correct date all along!

"Of course, we'll go along," she gently consoled between bites. "No more jolts, ambushes, or bumps in the night."

"Sounds mighty dull to me," Mabel grumbled into her tea.

"No exceptions," Greg reiterated. "Not one more surprise."

13

"OH, JANEY, I DO WISH Gregory had been up for just one more surprise," Mabel exclaimed in Sir's large blue and white tiled gourmet kitchen.

Jane was standing at the butcher-block island beneath a row of shiny copper pans, pouring sugar into a cut-glass pitcher full of lemonade. She sighed in pensive agreement.

It was early September. Labor Day, to be exact. Nearly three months had passed since Greg's ban on their antics. To Jane's relief, Mabel had left the subject of her due date alone for the duration of the summer. But it was the Barons' annual season's-end party, and Jane was in her twenty-ninth week. Reality was closing in swiftly with Jane's expanding belly, and Mabel was anxious to set Greg straight about the date of delivery.

But self-preservation was the only thing on Jane's mind today. In anticipation of the extended trip to England, Greg had invited his film crew to Minnesota for Sir's bash, to mingle with local society and get better acquainted themselves. At this moment they were en route from the Minneapolis-St. Paul International Airport, and would soon be joining the party in progress.

"Grandma," she began, turning to set the large stirring spoon in the stainless-steel sink. "Telling Greg anything today would be too much. I—"

"Sorry to interrupt," Grimes said, entering from the sliding rear door. "We need more of your potato salad, Mabel."

"Coming right up," Mabel chirped.

Jane watched with interest as her grandmother moved over to the refrigerator with a new spring in her white-sandaled step. The deeper worry lines caused by their discussion had vanished into her freshly glowing complexion. And wasn't that yellow dress new? Its bright, clingy fabric more reminiscent of Mabel's younger, more romantic days? She produced another bowl of her mayonnaise-and-vegetable concoction and set it in Grimes's waiting hands with more pomp than seemed necessary for potato salad. He nodded and eased back out to the flagstone patio, closing the screen behind him.

"You're blushing!" Jane noted in astonishment.

Mabel pressed the backs of her hands to her downy cheeks. "Must be a flash."

Jane gasped. "A flash of what?"

She lowered her eyes. "Oh, Janey!"

"What's with you and Grimes?" Jane grilled in disbelief.

"Oh, we're sort of flirty," she confided in a twitter. "Have been since the trip to Brainerd."

"Since then? Why haven't you said anything to me?"

"Because it's nothing serious," Mabel poohed-poohed. "And I knew you'd say he's ten years my junior—"

Jane pressed her fingers to her mouth. "There's that much difference in your ages!"

"Look at the gap between you and Greg."

"Touché. But what does Sir think?"

"Clark's just thankful Grimes has a new diversion," Mabel speculated. "Grimes had been playing out the health-watchdog role pretty heavily, monitoring Clark's every move. But it's nothing more than a movie and dinner now and then. Now don't try to divert me from our discussion," she said with a wagging finger. "Greg should be told when the baby is due."

Jane moved up beside her grandmother and gave her a squeeze. "I can't risk Greg's ire today, not with his ex-wife about to swoop in on her broom."

"I didn't realize she still worried you so," Mabel murmured. "And in two weeks' time they'll be winging off to Europe for six weeks! You kept this from him too long, Janey. Far too long!"

"Well, it's been such a magical summer," Jane offered in excuse, gazing out one of the large windows overlooking the back lawn to all the happy people milling round. Greg, dressed in navy shorts and a white knit shirt, was surrounded by his father's cronies, relating some story in animated detail. He was so darn happy right now. Settled in to their new life. Content with her. "Rattling his trust in me is going to be extremely tough."

"The secret will have to keep for a while longer, I suppose," Mabel clucked in agreement.

Jane's ample figure shook beneath her red maternity top and shorts. "Well, it's his fault I can't tell him today!" she suddenly declared poutily with a rap to the tiled counter. "Bringing his ex-viper here to mingle."

"Greg was no doubt hoping to ease the tensions between you by inviting her here," Mabel assured, smoothing Jane's wavy mane.

"Men are such fools!"

Mabel lifted her hands. "One of Mother Nature's little spoofs on the girls."

"I'll tell him first thing when he returns," Jane promised. "That will be sometime in late October, early November, leaving us a few weeks to buffer the blow before the baby comes."

Jane steered the conversation back to Mabel's flirty friendship with Grimes. They were still discussing it when Greg and Kevin suddenly popped through the sliding door.

"So here's the little flower girl!" Kevin greeted, his dark features alight with mischief. "You've grown!"

She fluttered her lashes prettily at Greg's director partner. "Since I played the flower girl?"

"Since my visit here last spring," he corrected, his brown eyes widened in mock disbelief as he surveyed her figure. "Greg's put me to shame with all the living he's done this year."

"Me too," Nicole bemoaned on a lilt of merriment that fooled no one, except perhaps the man easing through the door right behind her. He was a few inches taller than the statuesque Nicole, with large pleasant features and wheat-colored hair cut in Greg's shaggy style. Jane recognized him as Stephen Humphries, the prized host of Greg's English tour program.

Greg made introductions all around. The twenty years since Jane had indeed played the flower girl melted away as she and Nicole locked eyes. Jane swiftly made a thorough survey of her nemesis. The pictures Jane had seen of Greg's ex over the years had betrayed her to be quite militant and frill free. Apparently, as Greg had said, she was attempting to soften her image for the charming man standing at her elbow. Her cap of gold hair was longer than usual and she wore delicate silver jewelry at her ears and throat. Her choice of outfit—a ruffled halter blouse of transparent gauze and an aqua miniskirt—was not only feminine, but avant-garde. Perhaps she'd finally found her Prince Charming in Humphries and would lay off Greg!

But could she possibly hold on to a man as pleasant as Humphries? According to Greg, he was as charming as his television persona. Jane was convinced that Nicole hadn't changed one bit on the inside. Her eyes were still aflame with mean-spiritedness. That was the one thing that had hit Jane back at the age of five: the nasty glitter in Nicole's eyes. It was still there.

She felt a stab of pity for the likable Humphries, but it was swiftly overpowered by a sense of relief that he was smitten enough to divert Nicole's attention. He was well over twenty-one, probably closer to forty-five. He'd presumably been around long enough to see through Nicole's wrappings—a few curls, frills, and lipstick—and decide if he liked the contents.

Jane knew what she had to do. She fought back a cringe as she extended Nicole her hand in hospitality. "Glad you could come," she intoned.

Nicole drew a mocking smile. "You've grown quite a lot since we last met."

"Thanks to my Greg," she returned smoothly, though she felt as awkward as Dumbo the elephant.

Stephen Humphries chuckled good-naturedly, as he squeezed Jane's hand in his huge one. "I've heard all about your claim to Greg. I like a lady who knows what she wants early on."

"That is so good to hear," Nicole cooed, snuggling close, causing Greg and Kevin to exchange a look of disbelief. "I had better hang on to you tight today, Stephen, considering Jane's alluring powers." She favored Jane with a snide look that belied her sugary voice. "I am convinced she is a witch."

Just as Jane was convinced that Nicole was a bitch.

Greg could read it all over Jane's face as she bared her teeth. He angled an arm around his wife's shoulders. "Shall we join the others outside?" he suggested to the crowd. "Plenty of refreshments out on the patio."

Mabel took hold of the pitcher of lemonade and herded the guests back out the sliding door. Greg detained Jane, his gray eyes clouded with concern. "You okay? You handled her beautifully."

"I didn't even get the chance to really handle her," Jane muttered with clenched fists. "But I did win you, so I am the victor."

"I'm sure the venom is out of her system now, honey," he murmured apologetically, kissing her temple. "She's been waiting two decades for the chance to take a shot at you, and she pettily went for it."

"I hate her, Greg!"

"She's abrasive," Greg sympathized. "And I appreciate your patience."

"You shouldn't have brought her here!"

Greg smiled, tipping his forehead down on hers. "Honey, I always assemble my crews before a filming. It breaks the ice and promotes a teamlike atmosphere." When her frown didn't waver he exhaled impatiently. "I think you two needed to face each other. I wanted Nicole to see just how real our marriage is. And I wanted you to see exactly how unappealing she is to me. It would be awful to think that you were mourning my absence all the while I'm gone. It was important for you to witness the personal dynamics between all of us. Now you know for certain that there is absolutely nothing for you to be concerned about."

Jane agreed with a small sigh. "Kind of like a painful vaccination. One jab should take care of the ill."

"Exactly!" he rejoiced. "Let's go out there and enjoy ourselves."

Jane favored him with a jaundiced eye. "Seems to me that this is the picnic that you always bail out of."

He raised a palm. "I swear, no retreats to the hammock hidden in the trees. Half the guests are my age for the first time ever and I promise to stand by to entertain them."

Jane elbowed him in the gut, fully enjoying the fact that he couldn't return the favor.

Greg kept his vow to remain at the center of the action. He was so busy for the next few hours, passing out drinks and mingling, that he didn't notice Jane's absence. But when he did, he knew just where to look.

"I know you're in here," he chastised as he edged through the stand of pines concealing the hammock. He trotted across the grassy sun-dappled hideaway to where his wife was gently swinging in her large green vinyl cocoon. "Mrs. Baron . . ."

Janey's eyes fluttered open and she smiled dreamily. "That's me."

"You are a naughty girl."

"That's me."

"Why did you leave the party? Everybody from L.A. thinks you're charming."

"Almost everybody," she retorted, angling a hand over her eyes to peer up at his hovering form. "So sue me. I got tired of watching Nicole sashay around in that excuse for an outfit. She was trying to make me feel like a tank." She sighed. "Can you blame me, Greg? I just wanted to enjoy this Indian-summer day alone for a while. Think about nice things."

"Such as?"

"I was just thinking about you," she confided coyly.

He climbed into the folds of the hammock beside her, causing it to rock. "Oh yeah?"

"Yeah." She tipped on her side, propping up on an elbow. "Remember the time I kissed you back here?"

Greg closed his eyes and stretched his limbs with a low groan. "Of course. The shock took a year off my life! You were all of sixteen!"

"That was my first time."

He lifted his lids a fraction with a cocky grin. "I figured."

She leaned over to cover his mouth with her own, a pupil no longer. "Thanks," she breathed against lips. "For being so patient that time. All those times . . ."

"I've always loved you, honey," he crooned, raising a finger to her smooth cheek, "in one way or another. Guardian, father, brother. I've played all those roles along the way. It's been one long continuous adventure that's evolved into the ultimate commitment."

"I've just been lying here, thinking about our life together. Through the years, I mean." Jane swallowed hard, overcome with emotion over the new responsibilities awaiting them, and the circumstances of her pregnancy. "You aren't sorry, are you? That you married me, I mean?"

His expression grew earnest. "No, of course not. I've truly never been happier than I am at this moment. I'll be the second to declare—right after you—that this is the best thing that ever could've happened to me."

"Oh, you," she scoffed, pinching his nose.

"Seriously," he insisted on a lower note. "I doubted that I could deliver as a husband and a father. But our marriage has been so wonderful, so successful, that I'm more than convinced it was meant to be. The baby is bound to add further happiness to what we have. My only regret is that I didn't fall into line on my own, see that we belonged together for a lifetime."

"Oh!" Jane gasped with wide-eyed wonder.

"You can't be that shocked by my admission," he protested.

"No, no, the baby moved! I mean, really moved." Jane grabbed his hand and placed it on her abdomen. "Feel? No? How about here, or here?"

Greg chuckled as she guided his fingers from one spot to another. "Wow!" he exclaimed suddenly as he touched upon a sharp bulge. He pulled up her blouse without ceremony to examine the protrusion on her creamy skin. "It's hard to believe you're only six months along."

Jane smiled wanly. That crummy lie again. But she couldn't spoil this moment. It would go down in the memory bank as special. No matter what happened in the future, this one was a keeper.

"Hold me, Greg," she coaxed, wrapping her arms around his neck. "Just for a little while . . ."

"All right," he agreed, hauling her into the crook of his arm. "But only for a little while. A short, tiny space in time."

They rocked on for an hour, until Mabel and Grimes stumbled upon them in their bid to escape the masses!

THE BARGAIN BASEMENT was the busiest floor on the day before Halloween; so that was where Jane happened to be when she felt her first labor pain. She'd just rung up several purchases at the main register and was contemplating taking her lunch break when lightning seized her abdomen, slicing downward through her thighs. She grabbed the edge of the counter, gritted her teeth and rode the contraction through.

Audrey was swift to spot her trauma from the hosiery area and raced to the central counter as quickly as her high heels and tight purple shift would allow. "Oh, my stars!" Audrey proclaimed. "What's going on? Gas?"

Jane released a quaky breath, straightened as the pain subsided. "I don't think so."

"But it's way too early for the babe," Audrey protested.

Early, but not overly so, Jane silently corrected.

Audrey pulled a wooden chair out from the wall behind them. "Here. Sit."

Jane sank down with a sigh. "Uh, Audrey..."

She leaned over her with a pat to her orange hive of hair. "I've seen this happen many times to pregnant clerks over the years. A touch of gas."

Jane's creamy forehead furrowed. "This baby might be ready to come."

"Huh? Oh, you mean you might have miscalculated the date," Audrey eventually surmised, her tone weighted with playful implication.

Jane's lower lip jutted stubbornly. "It happens, you know."

"I know. But I didn't realize you and Greg were especially cozy until you showed up married."

Jane laced her hands around her tummy, her features paling against her frame of black hair. "Well, in any case, we didn't want our affair to be minced and diced on the store's gossip mill. I . . . just hoped that the baby would come later rather than sooner," she confessed lamely.

"Under the circumstances, I think I'd better call somebody," Audrey decided in a rush. "Who should I call, Jane? Little Sir ain't back from jolly old England yet, is he?"

"Call Sir upstairs."

Clark Baron was on the scene in minutes. Jane didn't know what to expect of him, but she was nonplussed by what she got. Clark Baron was the epitome of cool, polished sterling, from his hair to his eyes to his suit to his manner. Jane met his gaze with new confidence. Thank heavens he was helping her and he knew her due date to be only a couple of weeks ahead. She would have to explain nothing to him.

"Janey, dear." His tender tone blended perfectly with his dapper look. He knelt down at her chair and squeezed her hand. "Are the signs there? Backache? Cramps?"

She nodded. "Nesting, too. I cleaned the condo yesterday." A second contraction seized her then.

"Slow breathing, now," he soothed.

She heard him through her haze of pain, taking slow, light breaths. She took one last finishing one, as if to blow the contraction away forever. To realize it was only her second in a long line of them, made her cringe.

"Think of why you're doing it," Sir suggested. "The prize you get."

Jane eyed him dolefully. "Oh, you!"

Audrey glanced at her watch. "About fifteen minutes apart, I think."

"Time to go," Sir decided. He grasped Jane by the upper arm and eased her up. "Audrey, call security and make sure somebody hails us a cab. Then go up to my office, get the numbers for my home and Jane's grandmother. Start calling with messages right away."

"Messages?" Jane repeated frantically.

"Mabel and Grimes are at some old folks' home doing volunteer work at a Halloween wingding."

"And no Greg, either!" she cried in dismay.

"Don't you worry about your husband," Sir consoled, walking her toward the elevator. "I'll get ahold of him myself once we get to the hospital."

Jane blinked away the moistness in her eyes. "Thanks for being so ..."

He arched his brows. "For not falling apart? You forget, my girl, I'm a trained coach. Even though I missed the last class, I know what happens. I got Amanda to the hospital on time when she was in labor with Gregory, and I read a book on childbirth just last week."

Jane rolled her eyes with an endearing smile. "You Baron men sure have turned into a couple of bookworms on the subject."

THE DRIVE TO THE DOWNTOWN hospital was short and without incident. Sir deposited Jane in the capable hands of medical personnel at St. Joseph's, then retreated to the waiting area. The square bland room held only a few expectant family members. They were thumbing through magazines, watching the television mounted on an overhead shelf, or pacing among the rows of chairs. One thing they all had in common was their glazed expression, full of fear, anticipation and bewilderment.

Clark Baron could afford none of those things. He moved to the telephones banking the wall, extracted a small black book from the inner lining of his suit, and thumbed through the pages outlining Gregory's shooting schedule. According to the printed itinerary, he was at his last location, a village, by the name of Crickhowell. With the time difference, it would be early evening there, now. Sir dug into his trouser pocket for some coins and picked up the receiver.

"THIS LAST VILLAGE on the list has to be my favorite," Greg said to Kevin as they worked out their choice of lighting for the segment at St. Edmund's Church, a prominent Crickhowell landmark.

"Filming it at sunset will be remarkably beautiful," Kevin agreed, gauging the crew for readiness. "But I think this place is really your favorite because we're wrapping up the film here. You want to get home to your lovely bride."

In truth, Greg appreciated both the beauty of the location, and the conclusion of the project. He had been intrigued with this particular church even from a distance. As they'd rolled into town the other day, it was the structure's spire that had caught his eye, the way it rose above all the other rooftops. It proved to be such an impressive site, that Greg chose it to be the closing point of the show, with Stephen Humphries recapping his motorbike trip out front.

They'd filmed the old malt house and brewery yesterday. It was now converted into a craft workshop specializing in handmade furniture. He'd chosen a few pieces for the baby's nursery that were already on their way back to the States. Jane wasn't the only one who could spring a surprise!

"I'll get to the High Street tomorrow, include some shots of the Georgian facades in the closing credits," Kevin offered.

"Then cut away with a view of the towering Black Mountains," Greg finished neatly.

"That will leave you free to take the first flight out in the morning," Kevin explained.

"I would appreciate it," he confessed. "Jane isn't due for a while, but I've had the feeling all day that something is about to happen." He raked his fingers through his shagged hair. "But hell, it's way too early for any real news."

"Jane and your dad have the number of the Gwernvale," Kevin consoled.

The producer-director team was busy discussing dialogue with Stephen Humphries a short time later, when a boy from the Gwernvale rode up the street on an old bicycle. He'd had dealings with Nicole before, and went to her with the message.

Nicole's lean form, dressed in blue jeans and a brown silk blouse, went ramrod stiff as she scanned the paper. She frowned at the trio of men, standing at the stone entrance of the church, deeply engaged in conversation. Jane was up to something, she mused bitterly. She couldn't be in labor, yet. It had to be a trick, one of her showy bids for the spotlight.

Nicole's expression curled in scorn as she gazed out into the lovely green rolling hills. Finally, she was in control of their triangle! Jane didn't understand the importance of these assignments. But this was Greg's life! Her life, Kevin's life. Jane was an intruder. Nicole strolled over to Greg's loose-leaf book where he kept his production notes, and slipped the message into the wedge of pages. That would teach their flower girl a lesson. Repay her for being a lifelong pest!

Greg was exhausted as they finally called a wrap on the segment. He sank into one of the folding crew chairs and flipped through his loose-leaf binder.

That was when the message slip from the hotel slid into his lap.

Jane in labor. All's well. Don't worry. Just hurry. Dad

He absorbed the alarm, head snapping up to scan the area. "Who..." He trailed off in a mutter as he gazed around at the crew, who were packing up the cameras, grips, booms and microphones. It was a jovial madhouse, as always.

Except for sober Nicole. She was visibly tense as she said goodbye to Humphries, who was heading back to the hotel on the motorbike he'd been using on camera. As a matter of fact, she'd been tossing Greg small fidgety looks for a couple of hours, since the boy from the hotel had come on the bike.

She'd done this to him. With deliberate, malicious intent. Even now, as Humphries whizzed off down the street, she kept her distance from everyone.

"Nicole!" Greg's harsh summons made the whole crew freeze. No matter how tight the pressure, he never lost his cool this way. No one knew that better than Kevin, who was supervising the loading of the rental truck. He was close enough to spot the note in his friend's clenched fist, and fell in behind Nicole.

"What, Greg?" Her voice was cool, but her willowy body was quaking.

"You know what!" he retorted in a strangled voice. "This message! You kept it to yourself!"

"How do you know I—"

"Cut the crap! I saw the kid come to you."

"Oh...well..." she stumbled. "I didn't want to disrupt the shooting."

Kevin stepped in and pried the note from Greg's fingers. He swore under his breath as he scanned it. "Man, Nicole. This is a trashy trick, even for you. I'll race back to the hotel, Greg, pack your stuff."

"She isn't due for six weeks," Nicole protested. "This can't be real!"

Greg didn't know the answer to that one himself.

"It's a ploy to get you back home," Nicole concluded. "Jane's manipulating you again. You can't let her get away with it."

"What an idiot I've been," Greg muttered, rubbing his eyes.

"Yes," Nicole swiftly agreed with a triumphant nod.

"About you," he clarified tersely. "Being concerned with your well-being all these years. I've wanted to fire you dozens of times because you're so damn selfish and rigid."

"I don't believe it!" she gasped in affront.

"Why the hell not?" he roared back. "Don't you ever look at yourself in the mirror, woman? Peer beneath the surface? There's nothing wrong with being single at forty, but your track record with relationships is pathetic."

"It's bad luck that I'm still alone."

"It's bad behavior!"

"Jane's the one who's always misbehaved," she raved in disgust. "From our wedding on!"

"You're avenging the actions of a five-year-old girl?" he seethed. "Are you out of your mind?"

"All right," she ground out. "I am angry that she's succeeded where I failed."

"But you have Stephen now," Greg reminded. "Why didn't you just do the right thing and pass on this message?"

"Because," she snapped.

"You just had to take a whack at Jane," he acknowledged with reluctance. "No matter that you've found something good for yourself, you had to do it. Jane sensed your hatred at Dad's Labor Day party. But I secretly held out a hope that, if you just had a man of your own, you'd lighten up. But Nicole, you haven't one ounce of decency inside you—keeping a man from a wife about to give birth!"

Voices of shock and anger rose in the crew. They'd moved away from their tasks to listen to the confrontation. When Nicole whirled around searching for any allies, she came up empty.

"But she can't be giving birth, yet. And the note said she's fine. It must be a false alarm, don't you see? I decided the shoot was the priority."

Greg choked back a rise of sourness from his gut. Jane was probably frantic, wondering why he hadn't gotten back to her, to at the very least check out her condition. "You're through," he spat bitterly. "With Explore Unlimited and with me. Don't you dare step in the office again. Kevin will pack your gear and have it delivered."

"You need me," she insisted.

He reared back in surprise. "Like a dose of poison!"

14

GREG STARTED CALLING home immediately, but didn't manage to reach anyone until he was in the air, on a red-eye flight back to the Twin Cities. He finally pinned down Sir at the North Oaks estate, of all places.

"It was a false alarm," Sir reported with regret. "The doctor released her."

"But I called home and there was no answer," Greg objected, declining a sixth cup of coffee from the flight attendant.

"She's probably en route from the hospital to the condo. Mabel plans to stay on there with her."

Greg was puzzled by his father's disappointment. "Now, Dad. You know it's too early for that baby to arrive anyway."

"Oh, not really, son. A couple of weeks either way is common. Discussed it thoroughly over at the YWCA."

Greg inhaled sharply to cut himself off. In all the commotion, he'd forgotten that Sir still believed that Jane was several weeks pregnant when they married.

"You there, Greg?"

"Yeah, Dad. Guess I'm all wound up. Can't think straight."

"Thank the Lord you're on your way home. You cut this way too close, boy. Way too close."

"Sure, Dad. See you soon."

Greg replaced the phone in the seat in front of him and pulled a flight blanket over himself. He needed rest if he was ever going to sort out this confusion. Even more than rest, he needed Jane. As usual, she had him running circles around her. As usual, she would no doubt have a prompt and ready answer. But would it make any sense?

GREG ARRIVED at the condo at midmorning the following day. Jane opened the door just as he was inserting his key.

"Trick or treat?" she greeted, tumbling into his arms.

"Well, it's plain to see you're up to tricks, honey," he exclaimed, skimming her curves through her flowing white nightie with eager hands.

"Ah, Gregory!" Mabel's bandanna-topped head popped out of the kitchen. "So glad to see you back."

Greg smiled over Jane's shoulder. "Hello, Mabel."

Mabel moved briskly through the living room, bringing Greg's suitcase in from the hallway, grabbing her purse from the end table. "I hope you don't mind if I toddle off. Grimes and I are hosting another nursing-home costume party today. Happy Halloween!"

"Let's sit down on the sofa," Greg suggested, once Mabel was gone.

Jane showered him with kisses. "I've missed you like crazy."

"Me, too, honey."

"I'm sorry about the false alarm."

"Not your fault," Greg soothed, stroking her hair.

"I hope I didn't wreck your plans," she said in apology.

"No, of course not." He hauled her as close as he could. "Kevin's going to clean up the final details himself."

"With the help of the efficient Nicole, no doubt," Jane added in an effort to be civil.

Greg pursed his lips, fury simmering in his gut. "Well, no. I had to fire her yesterday. She won't be involved with me, you, or the company ever again."

Jane couldn't hide her joy. "Why?"

"Because she held back your message for a few hours."

"Oh, that viper!"

"Now, honey, don't let it upset you," he cautioned. "I'm just thankful that I didn't miss the birth because of her."

"That was a lucky break," Jane agreed, leaning over to pick through a wicker bowl of candy on the glass coffee table.

"Are you eating that stuff by the basketful now?" he questioned in horror.

"No, it's for the trick-or-treaters tonight," she explained, popping a piece of taffy into her mouth.

"I don't understand any of this, honey," he confided impatiently.

"It's easy," she said between chews. "The kids dress up, ring the doorbell, say trick—"

"No," he interrupted, tapping her moving lips. "I mean the red alert, the false labor."

Her eyes grew huge and she swallowed hard. "Oh."

"You aren't due for another month and a half—at least. Yet, you let Dad call me with the news that you might give birth any minute."

"I did have a few contractions," she hedged.

"I know it. But don't you think the charade has gone on long enough? That poor man believed I was going to miss the birth of my child, chastised me for scheduling my work too close to your due date. That made me feel terrible, Janey. Dad thinks I'm thoughtless."

"You're the poor man, Greg," she squeaked mournfully. "Not Sir."

"No, Janey, I didn't mean that. I don't want your sympathy. I can handle Dad. I just think we should set him straight. His heart is well on the mend again, he can take the truth now. He'll understand about the misunderstanding in your letter, about your allergic condition. We're married forever, that's all he'll care about."

"No! No! No!" she squealed in frustration. "You don't get it!"

"Honey, simmer down." Greg took her wrists and rubbed her pulse points. "Just tell me."

"But you said no more surprises. You were absolutely adamant about it."

"I remember. But I'll make one more exception," he urged softly.

"You're right about the charade reaching its limit. You are the poor man, Greg, not your father."

His jaw slacked. "Huh?"

Jane blinked tearfully. "Oh, darling, I've tried to tell you a hundred times. Sir has the right due date and you have the wrong one!"

"What?" Greg released a mighty roar, rocketing up from the sofa. "You were pregnant all the while, after shutting me down in Infants, after denying the contents of your letter? You were with child all the while?"

She cringed under his thunderous gaze. "Yes."

He threw his arms up in the air. "Guess we don't have to tell Dad another damn thing, do we?"

"No. That's one plus, anyway."

He bore down on her with blazing eyes. "I don't consider that much consolation, Jane!"

"This is just the kind of blowup I've been trying to avoid," she cried back. "I knew I'd lose, no matter when or how you found out the truth."

"Why did you do this?"

"Will you believe me if I tell you?"

"Yes!"

"Swear?"

"I swear," he said adamantly. "Give me the straight story."

"Only if you quit prowling over my head. Like you're about to lop it off!"

With a heaving chest, he sank down again on the cushions.

"I didn't know I was pregnant at first," she began. "I dictated the letter with the best intentions for my job. We'd broken up, remember? I had come to accept it. I simply wanted justice at the store."

He frowned in confusion. "So how did the pregnancy get tangled up in the letter?"

"Grandma has a special sight concerning maternity," Jane explained.

"Oh, c'mon!"

"She does. All the ladies in the old neighborhood used to come to her, to see if they were pregnant before bothering with a doctor's appointment. It's a reflection in the eyes or something." She watched his mouth compress. "You said you'd believe me."

"Go on," he urged with a wave.

"Well, she 'saw' the baby in me. And when she retyped the letter, that truth got inserted in the scramble."

Greg leaned forward, clasping his hands between his knees. "Scramble is right!"

Jane flashed him a pleading look. "She knew I was pregnant before *I* did, don't you see?"

"So just when did you find out?"

"Right before the wedding," she confessed in a smaller voice. "It was the main reason I accepted your insulting proposal."

"Insulting?"

"You know it was," she retorted. "Naturally, I wanted to help Sir out of his social jam, too. I didn't want to see him humiliated in front of his friends. But the news of a new Baron in the oven got me into that dress a lot quicker than anything else would have. I'm sure I would've done it for Sir, though, even without the baby... eventually."

"But I would've had to do some big-time begging first, I imagine," Greg inserted with insight.

"Oh, yes," she affirmed without shame. "You know, in a way, this was probably the best kind of beginning for us."

Greg shot her a blank stare. "Janey... I don't think that even you can concoct reasonable reasoning for this depth of subterfuge."

She smiled indulgently. "Look at it this way, darling. If you had known I was pregnant from the start, you might have been bitter over taking the vows. But as it was, you were doing it for Sir, and therefore grateful to me for helping out. You wanted to make me happy, remember?"

"Oh, yes, I remember, all right," he murmured, lost in a dazed memory of their emotional and lustful wedding night. That was an important point. Had he been angry with Jane, distrustful of her, he might not have made the effort he had. Then she, in turn, would not have responded in a lovable, kittenish way. They would have lived in a war zone, with the baby between them, forcing the bond. As crazy as the circumstances were, all had worked out for the best. As the baby had evolved inside Jane, his love had evolved around her, drawing them into a cozy triangle for three.

"And all I've ever wanted is to share my happiness with you, give you the family you so desperately need. So it makes perfect sense that I got pregnant ahead of time," she insisted. "I was guiding us into the kind of relationship fate had in mind all along."

"So after Mabel's fuss in the letter about rings, it's ended up in my nose of all places!"

"Hey, if the ring fits..." she said playfully.

"Well, that clears everything up," he admitted.

"Just like that?"

"Just like that."

"You know I love you, Greg."

His eyes crinkled at the corners. "I know you do."

"I tried to tell you so many times, but I was so embarrassed about the way I acted." She set a hand on his knee.

"Had I known how deeply and thoroughly in love we were going to grow, I would have confessed on our wedding night. Honest."

Greg wrapped her up in his arms, nuzzling the tender column of her throat. "All it really means, is that I'm going to be a dad a little sooner than I expected."

"Even sooner than that," she blurted out breathlessly as a contraction overtook her.

He was frozen in concern until her pain began to visibly subside and she was releasing a cleansing breath. "How can you be sure?"

"My water's breaking."

He nodded once, biting his lip white. "Okay. You're sure."

"So let's get going, dad!"

JANE AND GREG had a son before the night was through. David Gregory Baron entered the world shortly after midnight, missing a Halloween birthday by minutes; much to Jane's disappointment and Greg's relief. Jane figured the goblin tie-in would make the yearly celebrations great fun, but Greg had the feeling that having a mother as creative and impish as Jane was bound to be enough pressure on the lad's parties as it was.

David was a lightweight, tipping the scales at six pounds, four ounces. But he was hearty just the same, with his mother's lusty wail and his father's fair hair.

His other features Mabel and Clark dueled over the following morning as they all gathered—along with Grimes—in Jane's room, to have a chance to hold the brand-new Baron. And when they finished discussing his appearance, they lit on his name.

"A mighty mite," Sir declared from the chair where he was gingerly holding his grandson. "We shall call him Mite for short."

"Mite?" Greg repeated. "No way, Dad."

"Can't stop me," Sir retorted with juvenile impudence.

"Greg should know that," Jane lilted from the bed.

"His name is Dave," Greg insisted. "That's perfect."

"The name David has such backbone," Grimes declared. "I suggest you stick to it."

"I'm going to call him sweetie pie for a while," Mabel announced with pride. The baby began to cry all of a sudden, stunning them all to silence.

"I know who has the most clout in this room," Jane teased.

"Sounds like Dave's hungry," Greg declared. He went to his father's chair and took the baby. He eased the bundle into Jane's arms and slid onto the mattress beside them.

"Sounds like sweetie pie's tired of all this company, too," Mabel added, beckoning to Grimes and Clark. "Time for us to leave, I think."

Clark rose from his chair with a groan. "I think I'll go home and take a nap. These all-nighters are beyond me." He followed Mabel and Grimes to the door, pausing to have the last word. "Gregory, you speak to Jane about my idea."

They were suddenly left in a beautiful cocoon of silence. Jane opened her hospital gown and cradled the baby at her breast. He began to suck from her nipple like a fragile little bird. "What was Sir referring to?"

"Oh, Dad's offering us the house, in trade for the condo."

"But why?"

"He'd like us to live as a suburban family, I think. Enjoy the spacious tranquillity of the estate, play in the nice big backyard. For his part, he misses the downtown energy. And the condo is so close to the store. Thanks to you, he has a bright new outlook on the Emporium. A new lease on life."

"I imagine the estate is a lot of pressure. Upkeep and all."

"He also hopes to spend part of the upcoming winters down south in warmer climes—with you minding the store, of course!"

"Really?" Jane absorbed it all through weary eyes and ears.

"I'm sure what he'd really like, is to share both local properties with us—and Mabel and Grimes, too."

"Like one happy family?" she lilted, openly warm to the idea.

"Exactly. Life will be hectic, with my West Coast office and your new duties at the Emporium. I imagine we'll all have to work together to take care of David and keep the estate and condo in order."

"Ah, how lucky we are to have such eager backup."

"How lucky we are to have each other," he purred, kissing her deeply and deliciously. David cried out as his father nudged in closer. "Hey, Mite," he protested with mock gruffness. "You gotta learn to share with your old man."

Jane tipped her head into his with a soft laugh and teasing eyes. "Just when I manage to subdue one Baron bachelor, I find myself challenged with another."

Greg chuckled low and devilishly. "Now, mother dear, just which Baron boy do you think you've got tamed?"